GONE ROGUE SERIES

Rogue SURVIVOR

PATRICIA D. EDDY

Cover Design: Deranged Doctor Design

Cover Photo: Paul Henry Serres

Proofreading: Book Dweller Proofreading

For Abbie. My baby girl.

If you love sexy romantic suspense, I'd love to send you a short story set in Dublin, Ireland. Castles & Kings isn't available anywhere except for my mailing list. Click the link below and tell me where to send your free short story! http://patriciadeddy.com.

AUTHOR'S NOTE

I don't usually do this. Honestly, a lot of the time, it's because I just forget. But this book?

Well, this book is more.

More what?

More everything.

Connor and Isabel (and Veronica, of course) are going to stay with me for a very, very long time. I hope they'll stay with you too. I hope you love them. I hope you understand them. I hope I've done them justice.

I hope you have tissues.

PROLOGUE

Connor

THE SEEDY MOTEL on the outskirts of Dallas is mostly deserted. The only car in the parking lot belongs to the Bureau. I shouldn't be here. If Brent—my boss—finds out I appropriated resources for a *very* unofficial assignment, my career will be over faster than a duck on a June bug.

The two junior agents get out of a nondescript black sedan the second I park. They hang their heads, until the one on the left clears his throat. "The target is gone. We're not sure when he left. Could have been up to eight hours ago."

"*Eight hours?* You jack-offs had one job! One. And you fucked it right up," I snap. Thunder rumbles in the distance, and I slam the door of my truck, my hand going to my sidearm. Habit. Just like adjusting my Stetson.

The skies open, and not even the hat can protect me from the torrential downpour. "Fuckin' amateurs. Go home. I don't want to see either of your faces right now."

The two trainees—I don't even remember their names—mutter apologies, but I only care about one thing. Figuring out where my brother's ex—Alec—went when he left. Those fresh-out-of-Quantico fucks can't even tell me how long he's been gone.

I shoulder through the door, then clear the room in under thirty seconds. It's pristine. The only evidence *anyone* was here? An empty bag of granola in the trash. I *saw* the asshole through the curtains last night. Watching TV. Hell, I sat on him for six hours before I called in Tweedle Dumb and Tweedle Dumber to take over for me so I could get some sleep.

Shit. Whatever the hell Alec was doing here? He didn't stay long. Even the toilet paper on the roll is still folded into a little triangle. But on the bathroom window sill? Scuff marks. He escaped out the back. Did he spot the surveillance? Fuck. I *knew* I should have called in sick and watched the twat myself.

I stalk back to my truck, half-blinded by the rain and soaked to the skin. I need a Stetson with a bigger brim. Texas storms are no joke, and this one? It came out of nowhere.

Wrenching the door open, I'm about to climb inside, but pain explodes across the back of my skull and the hat tumbles onto the seat. Time slows, and the rain isn't the only thing obscuring my vision. Black spots form, spreading out until the lights inside the cab are nothing but pinpricks. A second blow, and they fade away completely.

THE GROUND RUSHES up to meet me, and I land with a weak "oof." Where the hell am I? Above me, the Texas sky goes on forever, but only a few stars remain amid the billowing clouds. I'm not in the city anymore. It's no longer raining. And it's too dark. Except for twin beams of light to my left. I blink hard. Headlights. Cold air rushes over my skin, and my head throbs with each beat of my heart.

Hotel. Alec. Ambush.

I'm only wearing my boxers and socks. No cell phone. No gun. No backup piece. Not even my pocket knife.

Shit. Think. Or you're fucked.

"You want to go first?" a gleeful male voice with a heavy Texas twang asks.

First? For what?

"Hell, yes." The second man is on the other side of me, but before I turn my head, something hard hits my right arm. The crack of bone sends white hot pain from my fingers to my shoulder, and I curl into a ball as another blow lands just above my knee. I catch a glimpse of a light, rounded length of wood, and by the time I figure out that it's a baseball bat, both of them are wailing on me.

Move! Do something, idiot!

My right hand is useless, but I claw at the ground with my left, desperate to get away. Lightning arcs across the sky, hitting a tree a couple hundred feet away.

The thunderclap shakes the ground, and the bat connects with my skull.

It's hard to breathe. Blood trickles into my left eye. The first voice is so close he must be kneeling next to me, but all I see is a diffuse shadow. "You fucked with the wrong man, Mr. F-B-I. Storm's rollin' in. I reckon you got another hour—maybe two— before you're so far underwater, they'll never find the body. And Quint...well, he's back where he's supposed to be. With Alec."

No. Anything but that.

My thoughts fracture. Memories so ephemeral I can barely hold onto them. Quinton when I rescued him from Alec's condo. His anger the last time we talked. How all he wanted was for me to be his *brother*. Not FBI Special Agent Connor Davis. Not Connor the Army Staff Sergeant. Not Connor the asshole. Just...Connor.

I'm beyond trying to protect myself. My head feels like it's full of cotton, and I can't fight anymore. My right side went numb a few minutes ago. Or was it longer? Rolling onto my back, I stare up at the dark clouds with my one good eye.

The pain fades with each blow. That's not good. I can *feel* the impact, but either there ain't much left to break, or my body's shutting down.

A fat drop of water hits my cheek. Then another. And another.

One of the fuckwits grabs my hair and slams my head against the hard-packed dirt. "Enjoy the rain, Davis. I hear Flash Flood Alley is the *perfect* place to drown."

With a last kick to my knee, they laugh, then get in their vehicle and drive away.

I'm dead. The blood flows thick and hot into my eye, and every few seconds, a fresh spasm of pure agony wracks my body. Each one weaker than the last. The stars are gone. But is that from the storm? Or my injuries?

It doesn't matter. Flash Flood Alley is in the middle of fucking nowhere, and unless those two shitheads left my phone around here—unlikely—no one's ever going to find me.

And in a few hours or less, this area of Texas will live up to its name. Which is the better way to die? Massive concussion and internal injuries or drowning?

I don't want to find out. But I will.

TOO MANY NOISES. Beeping. Clicking. Cold, gloved hands. Pressure. Pain.

Fragments of conversation I don't understand.

"...out in the middle of BFE..."

"...induced coma..."

"Quinton..."

Quinton? Where's my brother?

But I can't ask the question. I can't say anything. My throat is clogged, lips cracked and dry. It's dark. Or is it?

I'm vaguely aware of time passing. Long periods of silence punctuated by voices and the hiss of machines. Always unable to see. To talk. To do anything but pray.

More beeping. My head feels like it's about to explode. My chest hurts. Everything hurts.

"Connor? Can you hear me? Open your eyes." The man's voice sounds like it's coming from a mile away. Pressure—gentle at first, then firmer—squeezes my fingers, and I try to lift my lids, but I can't even tell if they flutter.

A second attempt, then a third, and finally I can see. Sort of. Everything's blurry. A dark head of hair. White coat. Someone else in blue. And all those damn noises. With each hard blink, the world becomes a little clearer. A little sharper.

"Welcome back. Don't try to talk yet," the man in the white coat says, shining a light into each of my eyes.

"Fuckin' hell." Goddamn do those two words hurt.

"That's why you shouldn't talk," the man says with a dry chuckle. "You were intubated for almost forty-eight hours. Your throat probably feels like it's been scraped raw, and it will for the next day or two. We had to put you into a medically-induced coma when you were brought in. Your brain was swelling. You have a severe concussion along with a whole lot of other injuries."

My limbs feel heavy as fuck, and from what little I can see of my body? Wires and tubes and bandages everywhere.

Quinton.

"My...brother..." I whisper. He's in trouble because of me. Because I didn't do my fucking job and Alec got away.

A third man—one I didn't notice before—steps out of the shadows. Tall. Built. Dark brown hair. "My name's Jasper Blade," he says, his accent pure Texas. "Formerly with the Texas Ranger Division. My brother, AJ, led the search for you. He had to handle some paperwork, but he'll show up here sooner or later. Quinton's safe. Your brother has some powerful friends, Connor. They found him. He's gonna be all right, and the piece of shit responsible for takin' him paid for his crimes."

Paid for his crimes? Is he dead?

"He's...?" I can't say the words. Not with civilians around.

"Yup."

Thank fuck.

I have so many questions, but the overwhelming need to close my eyes is battling with my desire—and ability—to ask them. When the doctor tells me to get some rest, I listen. But the last thing I hear? Jasper's quiet voice close to my ear.

"That asshole fucked with the wrong people. The guys who did a number on you? They won't be talkin'—or breathin'—again. So you rest up and heal. From what I hear, your brother's gonna want to talk to you in another day or so. Make sure you're ready. And don't let him down."

Two Days Later

AJ STRIDES into the hospital room with his tablet tucked under his arm. "Lookin' a little more alive than dead today," he says. "Ready to call your brother?"

No.

I look like shit. The right side of my face is purple, my eye bloody, and my arm held tight in a sling. My entire chest is covered in bruises. And that's just from the waist up. Surgery on my knee is scheduled for tomorrow. Total reconstruction. I can't hold a thought in my head for longer than five minutes, and the headaches...fuck. It's like someone's splitting my skull in two. But Quinton's safe and, much to my shock, *wants* to talk to me.

"Ain't letting him see me...like this."

AJ gives me the side eye. "Like what?"

"Fucked." With a heavy sigh, I pull the blankets higher. Can't exactly put on a shirt with a partially separated shoulder. "In the head."

"You have a concussion," he says like it's the most obvious fact in the world.

I give him my best "no shit, Sherlock" glare, but with how swollen my face is, I have no idea if it's effective. "Hard to think. Quinton...will worry."

"He knows what happened, dude. And of course he's gonna worry. He's your brother." AJ sinks into the chair and props the tablet on the table spanning the width of the bed.

"We're not close." My words are slow, like I have a mouthful of peanut butter. The admission drives all my failures home, and I drop my gaze to my right hand. Two broken fingers. Can't hold a pen. The splints are uncomfortable as fuck, but they're nothing compared to the brace on my leg. Or the contraption holding my broken right arm tight to my torso. Velcro and rough, scratchy fabric.

AJ snorts. "I know what that's like. You met Jasper."

Jasper. Who...? For a few endless moments, the name rattles around in my addled brain until I remember his words whispered so only I could hear. *"That asshole fucked with the wrong people. The guys who did a number on you? They won't be talkin'— or breathin'—again."*

"Yeah. So?" I ask.

"The only time we talk is when we're workin' a case. Sombitch nearly died last year and still wouldn't pick up the damn phone." After a dry chuckle, AJ shakes his head. "Then again, I didn't either. He's still my brother. I still love him. I'd still die for him. Even if I can't stand him most of the time."

"Quinton's hurt...because of me." The guilt pains me more than any of my injuries. If my brother hadn't started seeing some mercenary named Graham a few weeks ago, he'd be dead by now—and so would I.

AJ brings up a FaceTime window and pulls a Post-it note from his back pocket. "Bullshit. He's hurt because that no-good asswipe was fucked in the head. You're both alive. Nut up. I'm dialin', then I'll wait outside. But if I see you hang up in the next two minutes, my next call is gonna be to your mama."

Fuck. That's just what I need.

With a careful nod—my head hasn't stopped pounding all day—I give in, and when Quinton's face appears, the relief in his eyes? Maybe we'll both be all right. Eventually.

CHAPTER ONE

Connor

"Son of a bitch!" My left knee buckles, my foot missing the second step entirely, and I end up in a heap on the concrete landing of the FBI's Austin field office. Halos of light flash in my periphery, a side effect of the beating that almost took my life three months ago. When they hit, my equilibrium goes to shit.

As if this day weren't bad enough already.

"Connor!" My supervisor, Senior Field Agent Brent Wilder, rushes over to me, but I shake off his hand when he tries to help me up. "What the hell happened?"

With a grunt, I use the handrail to pull myself to my feet. "Wasn't watchin' where I was going."

Brent glares at me with the power of twenty years at the Bureau behind his eyes. "Bullshit. You want to try that again?"

"Nope." After almost a full minute of silence—a minute where I'm trying desperately not to rub at the bone-deep ache in my right arm or shift my weight onto the leg that just betrayed me—I tighten my hold on the railing and meet Brent's gaze. "You read my medical report."

"I did." He ticks off my various temporary and *permanent* disabilities on his fingers. "Vision loss in your right eye. Rebuilt knee, traumatic brain injury with occasional aphasia and post-concussion syndrome, shattered right ulna with nerve damage, and lasting migraines."

Hearing someone enumerate my failings does nothing for my mood. I'd tell him to go fuck himself, but that would get me shitcanned in zero point two seconds, and I need this job. For ten years, Brent has been my mentor, my supervisor, even my friend. When he transferred to Austin from Dallas two months ago, I put in my paperwork as well—even though I was still on medical leave. I can't lie to him. Even if I want to.

"Flashes. Halos. In my field of vision. Took me by surprise. Then my knee gave out." I stare through the glass doors to the lobby, the building nondescript save for the Bureau insignia inlaid in the stone tile.

"Shit. How the hell did you get the doctors to clear you for desk duty? Blackmail?" He shakes his head and gives me the side eye.

"Maybe." I crack a smile, but he's not amused. "I haven't had a flare in two weeks. Thought I might be done with them."

"Come on inside. We need to talk."

This can't be good. Brent runs a hand through his hair, then offers me his arm. Like I'd take it. I'm not helpless. At least not completely. After a deep breath, I take one tentative step, my fingers still clutching the handrail like it's my only tether to reality. Pain races up my leg, all the way to my hip, but I don't go down again. "I got it," I mutter and follow him inside.

Brent bypasses the stairs—thank God—and heads for the elevator. Three floors of awkward silence later, he unlocks his office door and gestures for me to sit before digging in his file cabinet for a thick folder.

"Connor, you went through hell. I spoke to the Bureau's physical therapist, and he's amazed at your progress. But cleared or not, what happened outside? You ain't ready. And worse, you're a liability. If you'd aggravated any of your existing injuries, if you'd hurt someone else..." He shakes his head. "I can't have you working in this office. Not even on desk duty."

"Fuckin' hell, Brent. Come on..." What am I supposed to do without this job? Without a reason to get up in the morning? "It was a one-time thing."

"Then go back to the docs and have them confirm it. But until then, you're on medical leave." He flips through the file until he finds a stack of pages secured with a paper clip. "Disability paperwork. Fill it out, send it to Human Resources. Then go home."

"And do what?" My hand shakes as I accept the forms, and Brent's look of pity? Fuck.

"Work your physical therapy, and when you haven't had any mental side effects in a month *and* you can pass the field agent physical fitness test, we'll talk again."

His tone leaves no room for argument, and thirty minutes later, paperwork filed, I'm back outside clutching that goddamned handrail like it's my only anchor to this world. Maybe...it is.

By the time the bus drops me off two blocks from my apartment—traffic in Austin is fucked twenty-four seven—rain is falling in sheets. One of the junior agents who *lost* my brother's ex at that hotel in Dallas three months ago was supposed to drive me to and from work all week. But I couldn't take him away from his caseload in the middle of the day. So now, I'm soaked to the skin, and the memories of that God-awful night I almost died in Flash Flood Alley play on a loop in my head.

The torrent of water washing the blood from my eyes. Shivering. So cold I couldn't feel my hands or feet. Then an eerie stillness. Peace, even as the storm raged above me. Thunder and lightning, loud and bright enough to permeate my last moments of consciousness.

"Stop it," I mutter as I drop my hat on the table by the door. "You're better than this."

But am I? My knee aches with each step, and I can feel the tight band across my forehead that signals an impending migraine.

Leaving a pile of wet clothes on the bathroom floor, I flip the shower as hot as it will go and step under the spray.

Six more weeks of disability. Mandatory. And that's assuming I can pass the physical fitness test. My body is a shadow of what it used to be. The soap slips out of my hand—nerve damage stole too much of my fine motor control—and I catch sight of the long surgical scar running down my thigh.

I haven't looked in the mirror since I got out of the hospital. Don't want to see my rebuilt knee. All the muscle tone I've lost. The way a single lock of my short, dark brown hair sticks up on the side from a subtle dent in my skull.

For months, I've done every fucking thing my sadistic physical therapist asked. And it *still* wasn't enough.

Tonight, I'll order a pizza and feel sorry for myself. But tomorrow? Time to start fixing what those assholes broke.

Isabel

The buzz of my watch startles me, and I drop the pen mid-twirl. It hits the yellow legal pad, and ink splatters across the page. "Shit."

No more fountain pens. A ball point wouldn't have made a mess of an entire afternoon's work. The grant proposal is due in a little over a week, and my old-school methods have put me behind. Why can't I compose an abstract on my laptop like everyone else?

Because you'd still play with your pen non-stop, and you would have just destroyed your keyboard.

But all those perfect words I crafted today would still be legible. Instead, I'll have to start over after Veronica goes to bed. What's one more late night? Long after she's asleep, I'll rework the whole thing. This time with a better pen. After I toss the ruined page into the trash, I sling my purse over my shoulder and head for the door. If I don't leave in the next ten minutes, Austin traffic will grind to a halt, and Veronica will eat dinner at Mitzi's house—again.

My job—Assistant Director of the National Second Chances Network—has kept me away from my daughter all too often these past six months. We're one of the fastest growing non-profits in the country, but all that expansion will come to a screeching halt if we can't raise additional funds.

I'm surprised our CFO, Luke, hasn't been in my office every hour today. The man wouldn't know patience if it smacked him upside the head, and I've been ignoring his emails all week so I could stay focused.

My cell vibrates in my hand, and I glance at the screen.

Are you going to pick me up? Mitzi's dad will be here in fifteen minutes. If you're working late, I'll catch a ride with them.

With a sigh, I slide my thumb over the keyboard.

On my way. You get to pick the pizza toppings tonight. xoxo.

I'm steps from the door when Luke calls my name from the coffee machine. "Isabel. Wait up!"

With a sigh, I turn, keys in my hand. "Whatever it is, can we talk about it tomorrow? I promised Veronica I wouldn't be late picking her up again."

His black hair falls over his forehead, and he gives me one of his million-watt smiles. "Sure, babe."

I freeze, and from the look on Luke's face, Mama would be

proud of the way I cut him down with just my eyes. "Good night, *Luke*."

Backing up a step, he drops his gaze to his shoes. "Sorry. It slipped out."

"Slipped out? Did you pay *any* attention to the sensitivity training last month? Women aren't 'babes.' You don't get to call me hon, dear, darlin', sweetie, baby, sweetcakes, or anything else besides Isabel."

"Um...right," he mumbles. "I'll see you tomorrow, Isabel."

Turning on my heel, I straighten my shoulders and head for the parking garage. Luke's great with numbers, and he's saved the organization hundreds of thousands of dollars since he took this job two years ago. But his penchant for calling all the women he meets "babe" grates on me.

Once I'm in the car, the GPS mocks me. The drive that should take twenty minutes? Today, it's over forty. My phone connects to the car's Bluetooth, and I tap the handsfree button on the steering wheel.

"Text Veronica. Message reads: Sorry, sweetie. Had to teach Luke some manners and traffic is tight as a wet boot. I'll be twenty minutes late."

When I pause, the voice recognition software asks, "Would you like me to send your message?"

"Yes." The whooshing sound of the text leaving my phone fills the small SUV, and I hope she's not too mad at me. Or stuck waiting alone. Her school is in a safe neighborhood. One of the safest. For what the Austin Academy costs, it better be. But when I took this job, I knew picking my daughter up on time every day would be a challenge.

"Text from...Veronica," the computerized voice announces.

"Play message." My heart sinks as the rain starts to drum against my windshield. This storm is going to be a toad strangler, and I know exactly what's coming next.

"Total downpour here. Going to Mitzi's. Pick me up there?"

Shit. One more parental fail in my column. We've always been close, and she knows how important this job is—not only to me, but to the people Second Chances helps. Still...how many times can I fail her before she starts to hate me?

"Mom? Are you listening?" Veronica asks over her third slice of loaded pepperoni. Oh, to have a teenager's metabolism.

Lifting my gaze, I smile. "Sorry. You could only reach four of the six names I gave you?"

She runs a hand through her long, wavy hair and frowns. "The other two aren't answering their phones. We even went to the sober living home. Maryanne Jarck left ten days ago and Nelson Gomez hasn't been there in a month."

"When did y'all go to Midtown? That wasn't part of the plan."

Keep your cool. She's sitting across from you. Perfectly safe.

Through a mouthful of pizza, she mumbles, "Monday. We were fine, Mom. The counselor was really nice and made sure we didn't bother any of the other residents. But Jamie—she was Maryanne's roommate—found us as we were leaving. She was really worried about her. She even went to the police, but they wouldn't investigate. I think there's a bigger story than the shitty—"

"Careful there, baby girl," I warn.

With an eye roll, she sighs. "I'm seventeen. In six months, I'll be at UT Austin and I'll be able to swear whenever I want."

Arching a brow, I give her my best mom stare. "Until then, you will watch your language. I taught you better than that."

Her cheeks tinge a dark red, and a part of me wants to tell her she can curse to her heart's content. But that would disqualify me from the Mom of the Year award.

Don't kid yourself. You earned a permanent ban from competition years ago.

As if to prove my point, Veronica hunches over her plate, picking at her pizza crust. Great. All that excitement...gone.

"V, tell me about the story. Please?" Nudging the pizza box closer to her—my girl can put away a whole pie by herself if she wants to—I offer her a smile. "I thought you were writing an exposé on the lack of resources recovering addicts have once they leave rehab?"

"We are." She straightens and grabs another slice. "But Jamie says there's a bigger problem. Someone doesn't want them to stay clean."

"What?" This was supposed to be an easy story. Or at least a safe one. The men and women who volunteered to talk to her? I vetted each one of them. Made sure they weren't violent. That they'd all been clean at least six months, that they had jobs and a good rating from the sober living home.

"Jamie said Maryanne and Nelson were doing well. Working their programs. Until the phone calls started. Day and night for over a week. And now they're gone. We're going back to talk to her in a few days. Before we'd finished our questions, she got a call and kicked us out."

"I don't think y'all should bother Jamie again," I say, giving up on restraint and snagging the next to last piece of pizza. "If two people have disappeared, that's a matter for the police."

"Mom. Really. It's not like we're detectives or anything. We're not gonna track Maryanne or Nelson down or force Jamie to talk to us. But we do want to see if Jamie knows who kept calling them." She swipes a napkin over her lips and sits back with a contented half smile.

Reaching across the table, I grasp her hand. "Sweetheart, please be careful. I don't like the idea of y'all getting mixed up in something...dangerous."

"We're just going to talk." Her eyes hold such hope, I relax my grip. "Nothing's going to happen to us, Mom. I promise."

CHAPTER TWO

Isabel

"WHAT ARE YOU UP TO TODAY?" I ask, leaning against the wall outside the conference room. Luke and Roger—Second Chances' director—will be here any minute to go over the first draft of the grant proposal, but Veronica was still asleep when I left for work this morning.

When I was her age, Senior Cut Day meant hanging out at the mall and sneaking cigarettes behind the 7-11. But she's nothing like I was at seventeen, and if I had to guess, she and Mitzi are spending their entire day off studying.

"After a coffee run, we're going to the library," she says on a yawn.

That's my girl.

"Nowhere else?" Our conversation about the sober living house kept me up most of the night. I'd forbid her from going back there if I thought it would do any good.

A heavy sigh carries over the line. "Mom." Veronica draws out the word, and I can imagine the eye roll.

She's seventeen. She's supposed to think I'm smothering her. If she didn't, I'd be worried.

"I'm just asking." Balancing my laptop and overstuffed file folder on my hip, I check my watch. Shit. I have to start setting up. "Coffee and the library. That's it, right?"

"Yes, Mother. *I promise.*"

"I'm 'Mother' now?" Chuckling, I give Roger a quick wave as he strides down the hall toward me. "Don't answer that. Just stay safe."

"We'll be fine. Love you."

She ends the call before I can tell her I love her too. Despite her theatrics, I'm lucky. She's a good kid. Always has been.

"Everything all right?" Roger asks when I follow him into the conference room and pocket my phone. Luke is already there, looking impatient as always.

"Fine. Just checking on my daughter. It's Senior Cut Day so she's not in school." Opening my laptop and connecting to the A/V system, I meet Roger's expectant gaze. "The grant proposal for the New Dawn Foundation is due in a week. I sent copies of the preliminary packet to both of y'all this morning, so if you'd like to follow along, you can. Remember, this is just a first draft, and we have plenty of time to make changes before the deadline. Ready for me to begin?"

At Roger's nod, I start my presentation. If I'm lucky, I won't have to work *every* night this week.

AFTER THE RUN-THROUGH, I close myself in my office and kick off my heels. Roger and Luke were thrilled with the draft, and while it's far from done, I can take a few minutes to catch up on my email before I escape to the gym for my lunchtime workout.

At the top of my inbox? A message from our Client Coordinator. She's responsible for pairing recovering addicts with our counselors, sober living homes, and jobs when they leave rehab.

Isabel, I checked the log files this morning and noticed something strange. Luke Overstreet accessed the client database four times in the past few months. He's not authorized to view those records. I asked IT to reset his password and restrict his permissions, but could you remind him why we limit the people who can view our clients' data? - Helen

Huh. There's no reason for Luke to be in those files. Only Helen and our counselors use the client database regularly. As Second Chances' Assistant Director, I have access, but whenever I need something—an address, a phone number, or demographics—I always go through Helen. Safer that way. My computer skills are only passable and I don't want to screw anything up.

Glancing at the clock, I slip on my running shoes. The impending lunch hour is the perfect excuse to get in and out of Luke's office quickly. The man leaves at 12:00 p.m. on the dot every single day.

He's reclining in his chair with his feet up on the window sill when I knock. "Got a minute?" I ask.

With a quick gaze at his watch, he smiles. "For you, Isabel, I have five."

It takes all I have not to cringe at his tone. At least he used my name this time.

Closing the door behind me, I adjust the strap of my gym bag on my shoulder. "Helen said you've been accessing client records. Any reason why?"

His eyes widen for a split second before the casual smile slides back into place. "Trina asked me to help her out a few times when her laptop was in for repairs. We really need to prioritize a mobile application for our counselors in the next fiscal year."

Some of the tension in my back melts away. "I don't

disagree. But next time, have Trina—or anyone else who asks—contact Helen or Sybil instead. We restrict access to those records for a reason. Our clients trust us to keep their personal information secure."

A hint of color darkens Luke's cheeks, and he nods. "It won't happen again." In the next breath, he's on his feet and reaching for the suit jacket draped over the back of his chair. "If you'll excuse me, I have reservations at Comedor on Colorado Street in fifteen minutes."

As he brushes past me on his way down the hall, I blow out a long, slow breath. Most of the time, the gym is a necessary evil. A way to combat the long hours sitting behind a desk. Today? It's an escape I desperately need.

***

Connor

The microwave dings, and I grab the burrito, only to drop it a half second later when molten cheese spills over my fingers. "Son of a bitch!"

Today has been a steaming pile of shit. The H-E-B was out of milk, and the rain started as I was limping out to my truck.

I knew getting up this morning was a mistake. Not like I have anywhere to be. Except the gym. For two weeks, I've gone every single day, but the halos and migraines? They're still happening. I can't lie to Brent—as much as I'd like to—and every time a flash of light fires in my periphery, I worry I'll *never* get my life back.

My knee aches when I kneel down to clean up the soggy mess, but my vision's clear today, so I give up on the idea of lunch and grab my gym bag.

Until I can earn a minimum of twenty points on the

Bureau's physical fitness exam, I won't show my face at the field office.

Before my injuries, I tested myself every few months and never scored less than twenty-five. Now? On a good day, I hit sixteen.

Thank God the doc cleared me to drive. Taking the bus five miles to the Central Austin Fitness Center every day was getting old. The end of January is cold, wet, and miserable, and the extra stress wasn't doing shit for my mental state.

After I stow my duffel bag in my locker, I drape a towel over one of the treadmills and drop down next to it, hooking my feet under the running board. My stopwatch buzzes as I reach forty-eight sit-ups. Not bad. That's a solid five points. But I only earn a single point on the 300-meter sprint, and by the time I collapse after forty-five push-ups—another four points—I know I've failed.

If I'd been raised with an ounce of quit in me, I'd head for the locker room. Instead, I set the treadmill for a little over seven miles per hour and try to outrun my demons.

Next to me, a curvy brunette reaches for her water bottle, but it slips from her hand and bounces along the belt. Her foot misses the hazard by less than an inch. I'm not going to hit my time on the mile and a half run, so I stop the machine and retrieve the metal container with UT Austin emblazoned on the side.

She jabs the stop button and offers me an embarrassed smile when I hand over the bottle. "Thanks. That could have ended very badly."

"Any run that ends is a good one," I say, and our fingers brush. Hers are soft and delicate, her nails painted a muted coral against her sun-kissed skin. What the hell? I shouldn't be noticing shit like that.

"You hate running? I see you here every day on the treadmill." A little furrow deepens between her brows.

She's noticed me?

Now it's my turn to be self-conscious. "Not by choice." Gesturing to the long scar running along my left leg, I grimace. "Multiple pins in my leg and a rebuilt knee. This is the only way I'll get my speed back up."

"Speed is overrated." Her lips curve again, and when she takes a swig of water, I can't look away. Flushed cheeks, minimal makeup, two tiny gold hoops in each ear. "Besides, weren't you over seven miles an hour? That's *fast*. I can barely manage five."

"Not fast enough." Grabbing my towel, I mop the sweat from my brow. "Need to be able to run a mile and a half in under ten minutes."

"Shit. Whoever's making you do that should be dragged behind a horse until they beg for mercy."

My laugh feels...good. Weird, but good, and I realize it's been months since I was able to relax around anyone. Hell, it's been months since I've talked to another person besides Brent and my medical team. "I'm afraid my employer wouldn't take too kindly to that, ma'am."

Now it's her turn to grimace. "Oh, God. I know you're just being polite, but don't call me ma'am. I already feel old enough trying to make it three miles on this cursed machine. I'm Isabel."

She holds out her hand, and I take it, my fingers dwarfing hers. "Connor. I didn't mean to offend..."

"This is Texas. And from your accent, I'd guess you were raised here?" She leans against the side of the treadmill and takes another long pull from her water bottle.

"Yes, ma'am—Isabel—just outside of Dallas. Only been in Austin a few months, though."

"Then it's in your blood. No offense taken. But if we're going to keep showing up here at the same time every day, I don't want you thinking of me as 'that old woman with butterfingers' or 'ma'am.'"

My throat goes dry, and a strange warmth coils in my gut. "Not a chance of that, Isabel." I doff an imaginary hat, then reach for my own water bottle. "Any labels you have for me I should know about?"

Crimson races up her neck to her cheeks, and she chokes on another sip of water, then presses her towel to her nose. "Hercules," she mumbles.

Shock silences me for too long, and Isabel's getting redder by the second. Before my wits return to my body, she snatches her phone from the treadmill's cupholder, and with her towel and water bottle clutched tightly to her chest, races for the locker room.

Well, fuck.

Fifteen minutes later, I push to my feet with a groan as Isabel passes through the gym's reception area.

"Isabel? Wait up. Please?" I spent every moment she was in the locker room trying to extricate my size thirteen shoe from my mouth, and I have to apologize.

Her brown eyes widen, but she does stop, though she's clearly ready to bolt any second.

"I'm an idiot," I say, shoving a hand through my hair, right over the slight dent in my skull. It's impossible to stifle my wince, and she takes a step closer, concern in her gaze, as I rush to continue. "You surprised me. I... My leg isn't the only part of me that's messed up. I didn't expect..." With a shrug, I stare down at the floor. "My mama would tan my hide if she knew I'd been that rude to you. I'm sorry."

"I'm the one who ogled you," she says softly. "Though, in my defense, you spend every workout doing more sit-ups and push-ups than I've ever *seen* before. Pretty sure if I tried even a tenth of what you do every day, I'd end up in traction."

"So...I didn't make a total ass of myself?"

Her smile lights up her entire face, and fuck. She's gorgeous. Dark brows, full lips, dressed in a pair of slacks and a soft cream blouse that hides everything—except her curves. "Oh, you did. But so did I. We're even."

Hold the phone. Is she flirting with me? The color dusting her cheeks and the way she's staring up at me, light dancing in her eyes, tells me it's a distinct possibility.

"Same time tomorrow?" I ask. "I can practice my water bottle catching skills again."

She laughs. A sweet sound, almost like birdsong. "Maybe? I have to sneak out of work every day to get here. This is the one hour a day no one needs me."

Maybe I need you. Working out is a hell of a lot easier with you next to me.

The thought is completely inappropriate, but my brain—and *other* parts of me—don't care. The few minutes we've had together? They've been the best I've had in...too long.

"Well, I'll be here. And if you ever want to try some push-ups—not that they're any more fun than the treadmill—I'll spot you."

Isabel's blush deepens and races down her neck. But a moment later, she clears her throat and smiles. "I'll leave the push-ups to you...*Hercules.*"

I'm too shocked to say a word as she gives me a little wave and heads for the elevator. The doors *snick* shut before I regain the ability to speak, and damn. I wish I'd been brave enough to ask her out for coffee.

CHAPTER THREE

Isabel

"WE'RE EVEN?"

"I'll leave the push-ups to you, Hercules?"

As the elevator doors open and I step into the gym's reception area, I replay every minute of yesterday's conversation with Connor—the one where I made a total and complete fool out of myself. The hottest guy in the gym. The one whose presence made all my workouts a *lot* more interesting. Or at least not so torturous. If he's here today, I'll have to give up my favorite treadmill—the one with the best view out the eighth-floor window. There's no way I'll be able to put one foot in front of the other next to him without falling on my face.

When I emerge from the locker room, I make it all of two steps before I see Connor on the treadmill. Yep, time to head for the ellipticals. Except he jumps off, catches my eye, and smiles, right before he drops to the floor for one of his epic rounds of push-ups.

Flames ignite somewhere deep in my core, and the sensation is so shocking, I almost drop my water bottle. Again.

Do not swoon. You're forty-six years old. Well past the age you should be swooning over anyone.

Except, that's exactly what I want to do. And now that he's seen me, I *have* to take my usual spot on the treadmill. After all, anything else would be rude. He grunts through one last push-up and collapses to the ground as I set my water bottle in the cup holder. "Got to make every rep worth it," he says, grimacing as he gets to his feet. "Since I'm the only one doin' 'em."

His wink takes me by surprise, and I catch a whiff of his cologne. Something soft, like sandalwood, along with what can only be pure *him* underneath. He hasn't been here long. Only a slight hint of sweat shines on his brow. Ten minutes, maybe?

He's still staring at me, hope and something else in his hazel eyes. A look I've seen before—every time I look in the mirror. A deep, abiding loneliness. Oh, God. Speak, Isabel. *Speak!*

"Hey."

Hey? That's the best you can do?

Can the ground swallow me whole now?

"How many today?" I ask.

The look on his face makes me regret saying anything, because now he knows I've been paying attention.

"Forty-nine. That's four points. Not bad, but not enough, either." Connor sets the treadmill for seven and a half miles an hour, balances on the side rails, and shakes his head. "Sorry. You probably have no idea what I'm talking about."

"I know you count your reps and write everything down in that little notebook," I say when I set my own pace at a leisurely three miles an hour. As much as I'd like to run every day—and my waistline would appreciate it—my knees wouldn't. Today, I'm going to be gentle with myself.

Half a mile passes before he curses under his breath and takes the speed down to a more reasonable jogging pace. "Physical fitness test. If I don't pass, I can't go back to my job."

"What kind of job requires you to run faster than seven

miles an hour? Jewel thief? Cheetah wrangler for the Austin Zoo? Olympic track and field pacer?"

A smile quirks his lips seconds before he stumbles. He recovers quickly, but when he slows the treadmill so he can walk next to me, he's limping a little. "I work for the government."

"City? State? Federal?" I should stop asking questions before he starts thinking I'm a crazed stalker.

After a long pause, he levels a serious gaze at me. "The FBI."

"Get out." I laugh, but his expression hasn't changed. "Seriously?"

He hits the kill switch on the console, and once the belt stops, pulls his left knee to his chest with a groan. "Yeah. Almost twenty years. Best job in the world."

"Except for the running?"

Shifting into a hamstring stretch, he chuckles and nods toward his rebuilt knee. "Maybe. Never had a problem passing before all this." His eyes unfocus, and suddenly he's grabbing onto the handrails like they're all that's keeping him upright. "Shit."

"Connor?" Jumping off my machine, I touch his arm gently, his corded muscles tensing under my fingers. "Are you okay?"

"Yeah. Just...done for today." He shuffles back a step, his gaze shifting to mine for only a second before he stares down at his feet.

There's that look again. The one I feel deep in my soul. "Already?" I ask. "Who's going to keep me company for the next two miles?"

"Sorry. You're on your own today. My leg isn't all that's messed up." With a single heave of his shoulders, he scoops up his towel, water bottle, and notebook. "I'm hittin' the showers. See you later, Isabel."

Before I can respond, he limps away.

Something inside me snaps. I can't let this man walk away

from me. Not like this. "Connor, wait." Leaving everything behind—even my phone—I rush after him, and thank God he stops before the men's locker room door. "Have coffee with me?"

His brows shoot up, but in the next breath, he shakes his head. "Probably not a good idea. I'm shit company."

"Oh? Do you slurp your coffee loud enough to wake the dead? Are you rude to baristas? Have you forgotten how to sit in a chair?"

What am I doing? The man said no. But he's obviously in pain, and in his eyes? I recognize that look. He's in Lonely Town. I should know. I'm a permanent resident.

"Well, no." The corners of his mouth twitch.

"I'm not a stalker. Despite all evidence to the contrary. I just thought...well...*I* could use some company. What about you?" Lifting a shoulder, I know I should stop talking, but I can't. "One...date. Coffee date. Err, one cup of coffee."

Shut up, Isabel. Why did you have to say date? Now he probably thinks you're going to hump his leg under the table.

This time, he smiles, and a hint of the loneliness eases. "There *is* a good coffee shop on the corner. I could meet you after you're done with your workout."

"Workouts are highly overrated. Coffee isn't."

"And what about dates?" he asks.

Oh, God. His voice is deeper now, and amusement dances in his eyes. I'm dead.

Here lies Isabel. Struck down by the embarrassment of asking a man out on a date.

Yet after a quick glance back at the treadmill and all of my stuff, I shrug. "With dates it can go either way. But I'm willing to bet you meet or exceed expectations."

Dead. Buried even.

"I'll do my best," he says, and my stomach does a somersault. "Lobby in ten? Fifteen?"

"I can be out in ten." I take a step back toward the treadmill, and he offers me one last smile before disappearing into the men's locker room.

You just asked a man out on a date. You. Isabel Lopez.

In nine years, I've had exactly three guys ask me out. I turned two of them down. One, Ricardo, lasted all of two dinners before he decided he couldn't handle the baggage of my then fourteen-year-old daughter. The daughter he hadn't even met.

Yet, not only did I flirt with a handsome FBI agent, I asked him out. I don't know who I am anymore. But...maybe I'll get out of Lonely Town myself for at least half an hour, and that'll be worth it.

Connor

What am I doing? Yesterday, I kicked myself for not asking Isabel out. But my confidence disappeared the moment I had a halo on the treadmill. What if I have another one in the middle of the coffee shop? Or worse—lose my words, my balance, my fine motor skills?

Anything's possible when I haven't slept, and nerve pain kept me up all hours last night.

With a towel around my waist, I drop down onto the bench in front of my locker and run my hands through my wet hair. One mistake, and I lost everything. If I hadn't been so pissed at the two junior agents watching my brother's sadistic ex, those asshole cops wouldn't have gotten the drop on me and I'd still be whole. Still be on the job.

When Isabel realizes how fucked-up I am, she'll run away so fast, I'll never be able to catch her.

And that'll be for the best.

Then why am I reaching for the cologne tucked in the side pocket of my duffel bag? Running a comb through my hair and actually glancing in the mirror inside the locker door?

Because you're fucking lonely, that's why.

It's one cup of coffee. A little conversation. A break in the monotony my life has become. And tomorrow, I'll get to the gym by 8:00 a.m. If I'm not working out right next to Isabel five days a week, I won't miss what we could have had.

My dark blue Wranglers and green Henley hide most of my scars from the world, and when I find Isabel leaning against the wall in the lobby, she smiles as she tucks her phone into her purse. "You clean up nice."

"You're gonna make a grown man blush." I hold the door open for her, and a stiff breeze ruffles her short black hair.

"Damn. I should have worn a better coat," she says, tugging her red blazer tightly around her. It's only a block to Beans and Brews Coffee and Tap House, but I take the leather jacket tucked under my arm and drape it over Isabel's shoulders.

"You're one of those 'gentlemen' I hear rumors about, aren't you?" she asks, shrugging into the jacket with a contented sigh. It dwarfs her, the sleeves easily three inches too long, but she looks amazing in it, and when she slips her hand in the crook of my arm, I realize just how much I've missed human contact. *Any* human contact.

"I cannot confirm or deny, ma'am." Tipping my Stetson, I quickly realize my mistake. "Apologies. Isabel. Afraid 'ma'am' was bred into me."

"You're forgiven. It's not the worst thing I've been called this week." She rolls her eyes, and I stop, covering her fingers with mine.

"Care to explain that?"

Isabel sighs. "It's not important. One of my coworkers thinks all women are his personal 'babes.' He's harmless. Just a jerk."

I don't offer to teach the ass some manners—even though I'd like to—just nod as we approach the coffee shop and she pulls away to open the door. I miss the warmth of her hand on my arm, of her closeness. Too much.

"Do you come here a lot?" she asks. "They're always busy when I pass by."

"This used to be my first stop every morning," I admit. "They knew me well enough to start an egg sandwich for me the moment I walked through the door."

Whether it's because she notices the sadness lacing my tone or my expression gives me away, I'm thankful she doesn't press, merely reaches out and gives my hand a squeeze.

After a brief argument over who should pay—that I win by telling her she can pick up the check next time—we find a quiet table in the back with our coffees and a chocolate chip cookie the size of a small dinner plate.

Isabel cups her mug and inhales deeply, but after her first sip, she stares into the dark brew. "I have a seventeen-year-old daughter." Her brown eyes flick to mine, and she takes a deep breath. "Sorry. I know that came out of nowhere, but the last time I had...um...a date with someone, he called me a lying bitch when I casually mentioned I had to pick up Veronica from her Model UN class. So now, I try to get it out of the way—"

"Isabel?" I reach across the table, my fingers grazing the soft skin of her wrist. "The last guy you went out with? He don't know his ass from a hole in the ground. We're having coffee. Not gettin' married. I'm forty-seven years old with a bad leg, a dent in my skull, and a disability check."

Shit.

Too much, too soon.

"A dent in your skull? What happened?" Isabel asks, leaning closer. She's not horrified. Not repulsed. At least, not yet.

"Couple of sombitches got the drop on me when I was working a case. I spent three weeks in the hospital, and now..."

"You're at the gym every day trying to get your life back." Laying her hand on the table, she seems to wait for me to take it, then squeezes my fingers gently. "So we both have baggage."

Chuckling, I pick up my coffee and toast her with it. "You don't get as far as we have in life without a couple of suitcases in tow."

If I'm not careful, I'll end up caring for this funny, beautiful, single mother who makes me feel like I'm not so broken. Right now, it doesn't matter that I could lose my balance when I stand up. That the chances of me returning to the FBI are slim to none at best. The only thing I care about is making sure Isabel leaves this date with a smile on her face. Maybe falling isn't always a bad thing.

CHAPTER FOUR

Isabel

STARING AT MY PHONE, my lunch all but forgotten in front of me, I delete the text on screen and start over—for the tenth time. Why am I so nervous? Connor's been nothing but polite, respectful, and funny as hell. After almost two weeks of coffee dates, we exchanged numbers, and though Veronica wanted to spend today at the botanical gardens, whenever she pulls out her phone to text Mitzi or post to one of her social media sites —all of which I follow—I message Connor.

She catches me peering at the screen when she comes back with extra ketchup for our fries.

"Mom, you've been texting all day. You *never* spend that much time on your phone. Not even when work is kicking your ass—sorry—your butt. Are you talking to a guy?"

"I...um..." I grab my diet pop and take a long sip to try to quell the burning in my cheeks. Why did I have to be so obvious? "Yes."

"It's about time! Who is he?" She leans forward, elbows on

the table, chin propped on her hands, and bats her eyelashes at me. "Come on. Spill it."

"He's just a guy from my gym. We've had coffee a few times."

With an eye roll worthy of Broadway, she snatches the phone out of my hand.

"Veronica! Do not read that!"

But it's too late. Her mouth forms a little *o*. "'I haven't stopped thinking about you since our first date.' 'Can I take you to dinner? I want more time with you than just the last half of your lunch hour.' Exactly how long has this been going on, Mom?"

"A week and a half." I'm dead again. How many times can I feel this...awkward in the space of a month? I'm so embarrassed my daughter caught me flirting, I wish I could disappear under this table and pretend this conversation never happened.

"You have to go out with him. Is he cute? Do you have a picture? How old is he? What does he do for a living? When can I meet him?"

"Slow down," I say, forcing a chuckle as I retrieve my phone. "He's forty-seven, and yes, he's cute. I do *not* have a picture because I'm not seventeen, and you will *not* meet him until we're a lot more serious than we are now."

"Mom." Another eye roll, this one accompanied by a long, drawn-out sigh. But in the next moment, she turns serious and holds my gaze. "You've been alone for almost ten years. Dad would want you to be happy."

A quick punch to my stomach couldn't have taken my breath away any faster. Tony's gone. Taken from me—and Veronica—by a twenty-one-year-old kid whose initiation to one of the local gangs involved robbing the convenience store Tony just happened to pick when our daughter needed cold medicine.

Forcing a slow, steady breath, I try to calm my pounding

heart. "I know, sweetheart. And I *am* happy. I have the best daughter in the world who, for some unknown reason, still wants to spend time with me on a weekend. I don't need anything more."

That's what I tell myself anyway. Most of the time it even works.

"In less than a year, I'll be at college. I know it's only twenty minutes away, but I'll have classes and homework and internships and maybe a party or two—I'll be safe, I promise—and you'll be free to do whatever you want. No more picking me up from the Academy, no more chauffeuring me to and from Mitzi's house, no pressure."

"You're an amazing young woman." I reach across the table and link my fingers with hers. "I love that you're okay with me dating, but I don't know if *I* am. For all the reasons you just listed. I don't want to miss a minute of your last few months at home with me."

Her little huff makes me laugh. "Fine. I'll make it easy for you. On Tuesday, Mitzi and I have to study for the AP English exam. We'll be busy all night. You won't miss anything because we won't be done until at least nine or ten. Go out with this guy. You can pick me up at Mitzi's dad's when you're done."

There go all of my excuses. "Fine. But you cannot spend the whole car ride home interrogating me. Deal?"

"Deal." She pulls her free hand out from under the table to show me her crossed fingers, but I can't be angry with her. She's right. Tony would want me to be happy, and while Veronica is everything I could have hoped for in a daughter, I deserve to see where this *thing* with Connor goes.

Pulling up his last text, I don't think twice about my reply.

"I'm free Tuesday night. Do you like Italian?"

Connor

Sitting in the back of the coffee shop—at what's become "our table" over the past two weeks—I wait for Isabel. We agreed to try a Monday morning date, and while I'll miss working out next to her, this gives us more time to talk. It's been almost ten days since I had a halo or any problems with my balance, and while I still can't pass that damn physical fitness exam, Brent agreed to plead my case to the special agent in charge. Limited desk duty would be better than nothing, and would get me out of my own head twenty hours a week.

Isabel rushes in, and I push to my feet. "Mornin', dar—Isabel. Got your coffee right here."

Did she notice I almost called her darlin'? I watch her for any sign she wasn't ready, that she took offense, but she leans in, hands on my biceps, and pecks my cheek. She smells like vanilla and something sweet, and her lips are warm against my skin until she jerks back. "Oh, God. I didn't think—was that okay?" A furrow appears between her brows and her body warms against me.

"Come here," I say, keeping my voice low. Sliding my hand from her back up to her neck, I draw her closer. Her lips are the stuff dreams are made of, and more than once this weekend, I imagined what it would be like to kiss her. Her taste. The sound she'd make—if any at all.

Gently, I slant my mouth over hers, and her fingers tighten at my waist. Every cell in my body wants more, but I don't press her, don't run my tongue along the seam of her lips, don't reach down to cup her ass. We're two consenting adults who've been around more than one block, but Isabel deserves my respect. Always. Even if my jeans *are* about to strangle my dick.

"Connor," she breathes when I release her. "Wow."

"Wow?" Pulling out her chair, I wait for her to sit before

taking a seat across from her. "When was the last time you were kissed, darlin'?"

Her hands curl around her mug, and she stares into the dark liquid. "Nine years ago."

"Nine years? Fuck, Isabel. You haven't kissed a man since…"

"My late husband." Her eyes shimmer, and she abandons her coffee for the scone I hoped she'd enjoy. Breaking off a corner, she stares at one plump blueberry. "I can't even tell you when it was, really. Not the night he died. Veronica was running a fever. She was miserable, and I was on the couch with her, trying to keep her comfortable. Tony was obsessing over the thermometer, driving me batty, and I finally sent him to the convenience store for some chocolate ice cream and aspirin." She falls silent, staring at the scone for long enough I'm about to clear my throat when she takes a shuddering breath. "I'm sorry. That was a lot first thing in the morning."

I nudge the plate closer to her. "I can handle 'a lot.' I told you I wanted to get to know you, Isabel. That don't mean just the good parts. My life ain't pretty. Now or…before. And one of these days, I'll tell you about it. Never thought I'd want anyone to know what happened to me, but with you…" I reach up and touch the depression in my skull. "Got no interest in hiding."

She stares at me like she can't believe I'm real. The feeling's mutual.

"The first day you asked me out for coffee? I told myself it was a one-time deal. That we'd spend half an hour talking about superficial shit, and then I'd disappear. Start workin' out earlier so I didn't make a damn fool of myself trying to be normal. But the next day, I couldn't do it. Showed up at noon again, hoping I'd see you."

"A one-time deal? Why?" Hurt edges her tone, though she reaches for my hand.

Holding on, her soft fingers against my rough ones, I pray what I'm about to do won't send her running for the hills. Carefully, I scoot my chair closer, then guide her hand to the top of my head. "Feel that?"

"Oh, my God. You said 'a dent,' but I didn't think..." She shakes her head. "I don't know what I thought. How—?"

"That's a story that needs alcohol. The short version? A baseball bat. Spent three weeks in the hospital. Lucky to be alive, lucky to still be able to walk, talk, think..." With a heavy sigh, I sit back and take a long sip of coffee. "Some days, I still have a hard time with all three."

"Shit, Connor. Are you okay to drive tomorrow? I never asked. Do you drive...at all? I could pick you up instead of meeting you at the restaurant." The briefest hint of pity lingers in her eyes, but she blinks once and it's gone, concern taking its place.

Finishing the last of my coffee, I want to escape. To head to the gym and run my problems away. But running would just make them worse. In some ways, I've been running for three months now, and I'm tired. So tired. I can't keep hiding from the world. And I definitely don't want to hide from Isabel. "Doc cleared me to drive last month. I can tell when I'm likely to get a migraine. That's when things get bad. You don't have to worry about me, Isabel."

She wraps her hands around her mug and holds my gaze. "I'm not *worried*. I'm...I care."

There's no deception to her words. I'm trained to read people. Isabel is as honest as they come. "I care too. After dinner tomorrow, will you let me take you to this quiet bar on Ninth? I want more time with you than just a meal. Time to get to know you. And maybe, I'll tell you about my brother and what happened to me when I tried to protect him."

Her smile, though sad, settles me and gives me hope I'm not too broken to find someone who understands me. Someone who'll accept my jagged edges, my scars, and most of all, my failings.

"I'd like that," she says. "Very much."

Isabel

Starting the day with Connor—and Beans and Brews' most excellent coffee—is fast becoming a habit I don't want to give up. Not even Luke's "Hey, babe. Any update on the grant proposal?" can dampen my mood.

"I'm submitting it tomorrow afternoon. Just need to polish the grammar up a bit and double-check the statistics I cited. I'll copy you and Roger on the final version. And don't call me 'babe.'"

"Sorry." He hunches his shoulders and heads for the coffee machine. I almost feel bad for chastising him, but his behavior affects more than just me. Every woman at the National Second Chances Network deserves respect, and Luke needs to learn that.

In my office, I pop in my earbuds and launch my *Instrumental* playlist. Three hours of verifying statistics is a boring—but necessary—evil, and I'll take all the help I can get to stay focused.

My office phone rings a little after 2:00 p.m. "This is Isabel Lopez," I say, my gaze never leaving the grant proposal on my laptop screen.

"Good afternoon, Isabel. It's Tracie Solis from the Midtown Sober Living Home. Do you have a few minutes?"

"Of course." The director of our preferred halfway house hasn't called me in months. I hope Veronica didn't pester the poor woman too much. "By the way, thank you for speaking with my daughter and her friend for their article in the Austin Academy's student newspaper."

"It was a pleasure. Veronica and Mitzi are both polite, intelligent, well-spoken young women. But that's not why I called. I'm afraid we won't be able to renew our contract with the National Second Chances Network for the upcoming fiscal year."

"Wh-why not?" Sitting up a little straighter, I grab a notepad from the corner of my desk and pull my pen cap off with my teeth. This is the last bit of news I expected today.

"The relapse rate for y'alls referrals has gone up fifty percent in the past six months. Every time a recovering addict backslides, there's a high chance they'll take another resident with them. We provide a safe, supportive place for our clients, and the risk is simply too great."

I'm baffled and scroll through the grant proposal until I find the relapse rate statistics I included. "I have the numbers right here, Tracie. Our five-year recidivism rate is less than thirty-five percent. That's the best in the country."

Tracie sighs, and her voice carries all the tension I feel. "Prior to last August, I would have agreed with you. But since then? Out of the thirty-two individuals you've sent to Midtown, twenty-four of them have left our program before their six-month graduation ceremony. At least fifteen have been arrested for possession—that I know of—and another three overdosed. The others...? I don't know what ultimately happened, but our counselors haven't been able to reach them."

This is bad. So very bad. If she's right—and word of this gets around before we submit the proposal—we're up a creek. "Can you give me just a moment? I'd like to check our records." I hate accessing the client database, but if there were ever a time to do it... I put Tracie on hold and bring up our last ten referrals to Midtown. Every single one of them has checked in like clockwork with our counselors. So why does Tracie think they've relapsed? "Thanks for your patience. I need to look into this further and talk to Helen, our Client Coordinator. Can I call you tomorrow?" Wiping my palms on my skirt, I hold my breath.

"I'm in Dallas at a conference tomorrow. I'll be back on Wednesday. I can't promise anything you find is gonna change my mind, Isabel. But I look forward to hearing from you."

The call drops, and I close my eyes, resting my head against the back of my chair.

Shit.

CHAPTER FIVE

Isabel

THE GLOW of downtown after dark mocks me from my office window. For the past twenty-four hours plus, I've been in panic mode. Helen has calls out to every one of the recovering addicts we've sent to Midtown in the past six months, but so far, no one's responded to her. At least the grant proposal is done and submitted, but if our numbers don't hold up going forward, our reputation will be worth less than mud, and we won't be able to keep providing the help this community so desperately needs.

My phone beeps, and I glance at the screen.

See you soon. Can't lie. I'm a little nervous. Been a long time since I took a beautiful woman to dinner.

My cheeks heat, and the low-level fluttering that's been my constant companion all day intensifies. Until I glance at the clock at the top of the screen. "Shit." I should have left for the restaurant ten minutes ago, but Luke put me behind by dumping a stack of financial reports on my desk this afternoon. Probably some childish retaliation for turning him down when he asked me to lunch today. If I don't get out of here, I'll be so hopelessly late, Connor will never forgive me. Or worse...he'll leave.

Veronica convinced me to wear the only "little black dress" in my closet and showed me a trick with a long red cardigan that turned it into a cute jacket. When I left the house, I didn't feel...*old*. But now? All my insecurities come rushing back faster than small-town gossip.

What am I doing? Going out on a dinner date with a guy who's easily hot enough to set me on fire? This isn't me. I'm Isabel the mom. Isabel the non-profit Assistant Director. Isabel the boring, middle-aged woman with stretch marks, sagging boobs, and crow's feet. Thank God I have a built-in curfew at nine to pick up Veronica. I'm terrified we'll sit down to dinner and suddenly have nothing to talk about.

My phone rings in my hand, and I stifle my yelp. Leah? Why would Mitzi's mom be calling me? The girls were supposed to be at her ex's place this evening.

"Hi, Leah. What's up? I thought the girls were at Brian's tonight."

"They never showed up," she says, her voice strained.

My world screeches to a halt. "They were supposed to go straight there from school..."

"Mitzi left her biology textbook at home, so I called Brian an hour ago. The jerk *forgot* he had her for the rest of the week. Neither of them are answering their phones, and Mitzi's is turned off. I can't even track her with the GPS app."

"Veronica knows better than to *ever* shut hers off. Give me a minute." Pulling up the website that lets me see her location, I force myself to take a deep breath and click on the *Find Phone* link. A circle spins in the center of the page for five seconds. Ten. Twenty.

Unable to locate phone: Veronica's Cell.

"Oh, God. Her phone is off too." Swallowing hard, I try to clear the boulder lodged in my throat. "She promised...after her dad died..."

"Isabel, something's wrong. I just *know* it. What are we going to do? Where are they?"

"Goofing off somewhere." I can't muster even a shred of confidence. Not for a second. Veronica was only eight when her dad was killed, but she still remembers that night. How frantic I was when a twenty-minute trip to the convenience store turned into forty, fifty, sixty. How many times I called his phone while she huddled on the couch with a fever of a hundred and two. "Are...are you at work? At the hospital? Can you check the ER?"

"Oh, God. No. No, no, no..."

"Leah. Listen. You have to check. You'll be able to find out if anyone was brought in without ID. I'll go home...see if they ended up there instead of Brian's. Maybe they started playing Xbox or listening to music and lost track of time."

"Y-yes. Of course. They're probably studying. Or something."

I don't believe that any more than Leah does, but every other explanation is much worse.

"I'll call you as soon as I check admitting." Leah's voice cracks, and she stifles a sob. "We never should have given Mitzi a car. If she still needed me to drive her everywhere..."

"Stop. Take a deep breath. Do it with me, okay?" This is my superpower. Calm in a crisis. Every crisis. Every scraped knee, broken bone, every teenage breakup or mean girl prank. But my baby girl...

Tears burn my eyes as I suck in a long, slow breath, then release it. "This is not your fault, Leah. How many times have we let them run all over town? Check admitting and call me back."

I leave everything. My laptop, my fancy dress heels under

my desk, my travel mug. Nothing matters but Veronica. I don't remember the five minute walk from my office to the parking garage. Only standing in front of my car unsure how I got here.

My hands shake, and I drop my keys twice trying to unlock the door. The moment the car rumbles to life, a wave of panic threatens to drown me, and I grip the steering wheel so hard, my knuckles turn white. I can't fall apart. Not now. Not here. Not until I know my daughter is safe.

"VERONICA?" Bursting through the front door of our single-story Craftsman, I know in less than five seconds...she's not here. The house is empty. Not just physically. Whenever V's home, her presence fills the space—every room, every hallway, every molecule of air. Now, the silence has a physical *weight*. A void that can't be satisfied with anything or anyone but her.

My phone rings, and I fumble getting it out of my purse. "Leah? Did you find anything?" My heart thumps so hard against my ribcage, I worry it's going to beat right out of my chest.

"No." Her voice is rough, and she swallows so hard I can hear it. "I called all the ERs in the city. None of them have admitted any teenage girls without ID tonight."

Shit.

"They're not at my house." Heading down the hall, I poke my head into Veronica's room. It's untouched, her bed a mess of fuzzy blankets and pillows. "I don't think they came here at all."

"I'll be home in ten minutes, but I called my neighbor, and she says all the lights are off. Brian is going to the library to see if anyone's still there, but they closed twenty minutes ago."

Swiping away the single tear that escapes the tight hold I have on my emotions, I sink down onto Veronica's bed and grab her pillow. It smells like her. Strawberry shampoo and that godawful perfume she insisted I buy her for Christmas. I hate the scent, but it's all that's holding me together right now.

"I'm going to the police station," I announce after swallowing the lump in my throat. "Report them missing."

They won't do anything. I'll be lucky if they don't laugh me out of the precinct.

She's just testing her boundaries.

Seventeen years old? Probably out partying. Or with a boy.

How are things at home? That age, most of the time, they run away for a night before they realize life ain't so easy on their own. She'll come back by morning.

All the things I know they'll say...so many of them variations of what they told me the night Tony died. Until someone finally connected the dots between the convenience store shooting, the victim without ID, and my repeated calls.

If Veronica were any other teenager, I might believe she was out partying. But her greatest act of rebellion involves cursing in front of me. She doesn't smoke, doesn't drink, has never touched an illegal drug in her life... My daughter loves school with an obsession that borders on unhealthy, but I don't complain. She's too driven. Too focused on college and her dreams of being a journalist to run away six months before graduation.

Leah's talking, and I shake my head, digging my fingers into my thigh and using the pain to help me focus. "Sorry. What did you say?"

"I can meet you there."

"No. You don't have security cameras at home. I do. My video doorbell records everyone who comes up the front walk. I'll know if they show up here. Start calling all of their friends. Let me know what Brian finds out when he goes to the library."

I hang up before Leah can respond. Before I lose my shit. Burying my face in Veronica's pillow long enough to let out a single, choking sob, I let her scent calm me. She has to be okay. I won't survive if she's not.

———

FOR THE THOUSANDTH TIME TONIGHT, I call Veronica's cell. No answer.

"Veronica? It's Mom. Again. Please, baby. Call me—"

"Mailbox full."

I checked her voicemail four hours ago. Nothing out of the ordinary. A few old messages from Mitzi, one from me telling her how proud I was of her for getting in to UT Austin, and one from Tracie, the woman who runs the sober living home.

"Veronica, Jamie hasn't been here for three days and she's not answering her phone. I had to reassign her room. If you hear from her, please let her know I'm sorry."

I tried calling Tracie, but not until well after 11:00 p.m., so she probably won't get back to me until the morning. What the hell am I supposed to do now? Besides delete some of the more than twenty messages I've left Veronica tonight. The police were exactly as much help as I predicted, and Leah's checking the local hospitals every few hours.

I haven't left Veronica's room since I got home from the precinct. I can't. If I thought it would do any good, I'd drive up and down every single street in Austin, but then I could miss her coming home.

If she comes home.

Pulling her purple fuzzy blanket around me, I lie on her bed, my phone still clutched in my hand. The ringer is set as loud as it can go, and it's fully charged. More than once tonight I've wondered if it's working, but Connor's called three times, so it must be. I let each one go to voicemail, though. What if Veronica called at the same time? The risk was too great.

"Please come back," I whisper when I close my eyes. "Wherever you are...just come home."

"Is this Isabel Lopez?" the tired, female voice asks. Seconds ago, the ringing phone woke me from a nightmare where ten years had passed with no sign of Veronica or Mitzi, and it took me several deep breaths to stop crying enough to see the caller ID. Austin Mercy Hospital.

"Y-yes. Please tell me my baby girl is okay. Veronica Lopez?" Sitting up, I sway against the headboard.

"Yes, ma'am. We admitted an unidentified female a little after 10:00 p.m. tonight. She was unconscious and needed surgery for a ruptured spleen and minor internal bleeding. She woke up a few minutes ago and was able to give us her name and your number. "

"Oh, God. Is she going to be all right?" I push to my feet, and a wave of dizziness threatens to send me back down to the bed. Shit. What time is it, anyway? A quick glance at my watch has me gaping. Almost 5:00 a.m.

"I'm only the charge nurse, ma'am. I can tell you that she's out of the woods for now and stable, but you really need to come in and discuss her condition with her doctor. She'll need your support and we need your permission for any further treatment she receives."

"Tell her...can you tell her I'm on my way? If she wakes up, I mean." Tears race down my cheeks, and I don't even try to stop them. My baby girl's alive. Oh, shit. What about Mitzi?

"I can—"

"Was there another girl brought in with her?" I ask. "Same age. Blond, blue eyes, five-foot-six?"

"We don't have any other unidentified females at the

moment, ma'am. I'm sorry. I have to go." The woman hangs up, and I realize I never got her name. Does it matter? Veronica's alive. I just hope alive also means...okay.

CHAPTER SIX

Isabel

My eyes burn, and the hard plastic chair in Veronica's hospital room isn't doing my back any favors. But I don't care. I'd sit on a bed of nails holding fifty pound weights if it would make Veronica better.

Concussion. Broken arm. Dislocated knee. Ruptured spleen.

She's only woken up for a few minutes at a time. Long enough to tell me she was sorry. To ask about Mitzi—and cry when I couldn't give her an answer. I should try to sleep. But I'm terrified I won't hear her quiet whispers. She had a terrible reaction to the painkiller they gave her when she first woke up, and the doctor warned me she'll likely sleep most of the day.

My bladder won't be ignored much longer, and I stifle my hiss when I push to my feet. I'm too old to stay up all night—let alone for almost thirty-six hours straight. Bracing my hands on either side of Veronica's shoulders, I press a kiss to her cheek. "Be right back, baby girl. Don't go anywhere, okay?"

She'd laugh—if she could hear me. Then say something

like, *"I don't know, Mom. I hear these beds can move pretty fast on freshly waxed floors."*

In the attached bathroom, I take care of my needs, then splash some cold water on my face. A quick glance in the mirror confirms I look like death warmed over, but I don't care. Veronica's alive. She'll heal.

Guilt threatens to choke me, stealing the few blessed moments of relief I'd found watching my daughter sleep. Mitzi is still out there somewhere. Is she hurt? Cold? Alone? And why didn't they go to Brian's after the library? I tried to ask Veronica what happened, but she teared up and her heart rate started to spike, so I backed off.

Dropping to my knees, I press my hands to my mouth, stifling my sobs. If I weren't so worried about Veronica, so keyed in to her every breath, so obsessed with every number on the machines monitoring her vitals, I'd call Leah. But what would I say?

"I'm sorry my daughter's safe?"

"I'm sorry yours isn't?"

I'm a horrible person.

That single thought helps me choke back the tears. After a few deep breaths, I swipe at my cheeks. I can't let Veronica see me cry. Not when she's so weak and raw. Sniffling, I pad back into her room but stop when I see a police officer standing just inside the door.

"Hello?" I say quietly. "Can I help you?"

"Ma'am." The man nods, his face sober. "I'm Officer Walter Milton with the Austin Police Department. I have some questions for your daughter."

I motion to the door, but the officer doesn't move. Really? "My daughter is resting. She's in no shape to answer questions right now."

"I'm afraid it can't wait, Mrs. Lopez."

"*Ms.* Lopez. And yes, it can." Standing between the officer and Veronica's bed, I set my hands on my hips. "If you have a card, I'll call you when she's up to talking."

"Mom?" My daughter's whisper has me whirling around and rushing to her side. "Is there water?"

"Yes, baby girl. Here you go." My hands shake as I angle the straw to her lips. She manages a couple small sips before I sense Officer Milton hovering right behind me.

"Veronica Lopez? I need to talk to you about your car accident."

Her eyes widen, and she chokes on the last of the water. Her face twists in pain when she coughs, and tears gather at the corners of her eyes.

"Back off," I snap, glaring at him. "I told you she isn't ready for this."

A nurse bursts in to the room and makes a beeline for Veronica. "What in heaven's name is going on in here?" she asks. "Are you okay, sweetie?"

"Y-yes." Veronica reaches for my hand, but I had to move out of the nurse's way, and she starts to cry harder. "Don't make me talk about the accident...please?"

Skirting the bed, I touch her shoulder, the thin hospital gown scratchy under my fingers. "Of course you don't have to talk about it. You just rest."

Officer Milton is still staring at my daughter, and I'm about to threaten to drag him out behind the barn and stick my foot up his ass when he pulls a card from his pocket and drops it on the foot of her bed. "I expect to hear from you in the next twenty-four hours, *Ms.* Lopez."

"Oh, your supervisor will hear from me," I mutter as soon as the door closes with him on the other side. "Coming in here like you own the place..."

The nurse—I think her name is Sheila—clucks her tongue. "He needs to be taught some manners." Turning her attention to Veronica, she smiles. "How's your pain level, sweetie? Scale of one to ten?"

"Four? Just tired." Her eyes flutter closed, and I lean down and press a kiss to her forehead. The scent of antiseptic clings to her, like it does to everything in this place. I wish I could take her home. Put her in her own bed and keep her safe for the rest of her life. But she needs to stay overnight. Just in case she has another reaction to her pain medication.

"Sleep, baby girl. I'll be here."

Nurse Sheila promises to check on us in another couple of hours, and I return to the hard plastic chair. After a few minutes, Veronica clears her throat. "I got on the wrong bus. That's—" she shudders, "—why I was on MLK."

"Where was Mitzi? She had her car. Y'all were supposed to be together the whole night." I hate the judgement in my tone. V doesn't need me berating her right now, no matter how confused—and yes, angry—I am.

The dark red tinge to her cheeks makes my guilt skyrocket, as does her wince when she tries to shift in the bed to get more comfortable. "I don't know. Couldn't find her...when the library closed. "

"Her mom's so worried, V. She can't track Mitzi's phone, the police haven't found her car. Are you *sure* you don't have any idea where she could have gone?"

A fresh trail of tears seeps onto the pillow, and Veronica shakes her head before she turns away from me. "I'm so sorry..."

"Shhh. It's all right. Just rest now."

Connor

Fuck it. Five points short of a passing grade on the Bureau's physical fitness test. My shoulder gave out after ten pull-ups and my knee buckled with a quarter mile left on my run.

After being stood up last night and having Isabel ghost me, failing—yet again—at the gym leaves me in the foulest mood imaginable. The only thing that can save today? A jalapeño and cheese Whataburger®.

I'm halfway through the meal when my cell phone rings. Brent's the last person I want to talk to right now, and I send the call to voicemail so I can eat in peace. But he's persistent as fuck and calls two more times before I finish my fries.

"What do you want?" The moment the words leave my mouth, I wince.

A sigh carries over the line. "Guess I was a fool for thinkin' time off would soften you. Seems it's made you even pricklier."

"Bad day at the gym."

"You up to twenty points yet?"

"If I were, do you think it would have been a *bad* day at the gym?" Snorting, I trudge into the kitchen for a cold glass of water. Each step feels like my running shoes are made of concrete—or lead. "Why are you calling? I need a shower."

He sighs again, and I can picture him now. Sitting at his desk staring out over the cubicles, weariness pressing down on his shoulders. "Orders came down an hour ago. I need to bring in your replacement."

The glass falls from my hand, shattering into a dozen pieces in the sink. "You told me filing for disability wouldn't put my job at risk. Pretty sure we have laws against this sort of thing."

"For fuck's sake," Brent mutters. "I'd have you back here in an hour if I could. But until your doc clears you *and* you can pass the fitness test, you're on leave, and we're understaffed. It's not permanent. Yet."

"Yet." Grabbing a fresh glass, I turn on the tap. "Give me a fuckin' honest answer, Brent. I'm tired and, thanks to you, I have a mess to clean up. Is there *any* chance I'll see field work again?"

He pauses for so long I have my answer.

"Great. Well, this has been a shit twenty-four hours. Reckon I'll just drop off my ID and gun by the end of the week, then."

"Don't. I'm tryin', Connor. I'd keep your desk empty for a year if I could, but every field office in Texas was stretched too thin *before* you were hurt. Once the new agent is selected, he or she is guaranteed a three-month placement. You can still come back, and I won't stop fighting to get you reinstated unless you tell me to. Deal?"

"I'll think about it." Jabbing the screen, I hang up before I say something I'll regret. Like telling my boss he can go fuck himself.

***

AN HOUR LATER, my phone buzzes again, and this time, I'm not holding back. Brent can go to hell if he thinks—shit. It's Isabel. I left her three messages last night, and when she didn't reply to any of them, I figured she'd come to her senses and rabbited. Can't say I blamed her.

"Connor?" She sounds tired. Exhausted, even. Her voice is rough, almost sultry, and my dick twitches against my zipper before worry takes over.

"I'm here, darlin'. What happened last night? I waited at the restaurant for an hour—"

"I know. I got your messages. Um...it's just...shit."

"Take a deep breath for me. Can you do that?" I run a hand through my hair, tugging at a few of the strands. If she's hurt, I'm a goddamn asshole for thinking she purposely stood me up. Hell, I'm probably an asshole even if she's fine. But the woman on the other end of the phone is definitely *not* fine.

She exhales and clears her throat. "My daughter...she went missing last night. All night, I didn't hear anything until 5:00 a.m. She's in the hospital. Someone hit my baby girl with their car and...and..."

"Slow down, Isabel. Is Veronica gonna be okay?" How could I have ever been angry with her? Fuck. If I'd known Quinton was missing before those two assholes got the jump on me, I would have moved the fucking world to get to him and ignored *everything* else in my life until he was safe.

"Y-yes. She...broken wrist, concussion. And they had to remove her spleen. She's sleeping right now. I need to get back to her, but I didn't want you to think...I wanted to call you last night—or answer when you called—but..."

"You had to keep the line open. Don't apologize, darlin'. Ain't no need. Just tell me what I can do to help."

"Nothing. Really," she says, and from the edge to her voice, she's barely holding it together.

"Have you eaten? Anything? I know how bad hospital food can be. Can I bring you dinner? I won't stay. Just drop somethin' off and let you be."

She makes a noise that might be a sob, and I wish I could put my arms around her and tell her everything was going to be okay. If this city didn't have at least ten different hospitals, I wouldn't have asked. Just showed up with as many different types of takeout as I could find on the way.

"Is that a yes?"

"We're at Austin Mercy Hospital," she says quietly. "Room 1131."

"Go back to Veronica, darlin'. I'll be there in an hour. " A meal isn't enough. It doesn't matter that we're new. That we've only shared a handful of kisses. She's hurting, and I'll do anything I can to make it better.

CHAPTER SEVEN

Connor

OUTSIDE ROOM 1131, I pause, two huge bags of takeout clutched in my hand. I had to flash my credentials at the nurse's station —the credentials that probably ain't worth spit anymore—but at least they got me in here. I stare through the narrow pane of glass in the door to Veronica's room. A privacy screen hides the bed from view, but Isabel slumps back in one of the unforgiving visitor chairs, her hand over her eyes.

Memories hit me, and I brace my arm on the wall when my bad knee threatens to buckle. Being unable to *think*, stumbling over my words, almost collapsing from dizziness the first time I tried to get from my hospital bed to the bathroom.

When I was discharged, I vowed I'd never set foot in another hospital. But Isabel's alone, and that's worth reliving my memories a thousand times.

Rapping my knuckles softly on the glass, I curse when she jerks up and cranes her neck in my direction. I didn't mean to startle her. But that smile she gives me? The relief in her eyes? I've never seen anything more beautiful.

"I can't believe you came," she says as she steps out into the hall.

Setting the bags on a bench, I wrap my arms around her. "Nowhere else I'd rather be right now. Plus, I owe you dinner."

Her weak chuckle does nothing to reassure me. "I'm still dressed for it. Mostly. Afraid my makeup didn't survive, though."

Drawing back to cup her cheek, I skate my thumb just under her left eye. Over the smudge of mascara and the puffy skin from crying. "I don't care. You're gorgeous, with or without makeup."

"And you're a good liar." She leans into my touch with a sigh. "I'm one step up from a zombie. I think I caught an hour between crying and pacing and calling the police so many times they threatened to arrest me for harassment."

Before I can ask who was that rude to her, she clutches the front of my flannel shirt and buries her face against my chest. I don't understand what's happening until her whole body starts to shake.

I've comforted more than a few women—both on the job and in my personal life—but this feels different. Isabel clings to me like I'm all that's holding her together. Her tears soak into my collar, and though I'll pay for this move later, I scoop her up and limp over to the bench so I can sit with her in my lap.

"I'm sorry," she sobs. "This isn't...me..."

"Darlin', I wouldn't trust anyone who didn't lose their shit in this situation. One of these days, I'll tell you what happened with my brother. When I found out someone was hurtin' him. Not proud of what I did back then, but wouldn't change a thing."

She sniffles, then swipes at her cheek. "I refuse to believe you did anything to be ashamed of."

Chuckling, I pull out a handkerchief and press it into her hand. "I broke the sombitch's door and punched him in the face. And I *might* have sent his boss—at the time—a copy of the protective order against him."

"Sounds like he deserved it." Isabel wipes away her tears and peers up at me. "And I want to hear the whole story. When..." With a quick glance at the door, all the tension returns to her body.

"I didn't mean to keep you," I say, helping her to her feet. "Will you call me when you can? After Veronica's home."

"Tomorrow. They're discharging her tomorrow." Isabel takes another look through the narrow window, then turns back to me and rests her palm over my heart. "Will you wait here for a minute? Please?"

"Yes, ma'am." She could ask me for the world, and I'd get it for her. Or die trying. I don't know why. We're so new, but I haven't felt this comfortable with a woman in years—if ever— or wanted more so quickly.

Isabel pokes her head out the door sixty seconds later and offers me a weary smile. "Come on in."

"Are you sure?"

"Veronica wants to meet you." She steps into the hall again and lowers her voice. "Mitzi's still missing, Connor. Her best friend. The police are finally looking for her, but V feels so guilty she can't think about anything else. You'll be a good distraction. Come in and say hi."

"She should rest—"

"Try telling a seventeen-year-old to take a nap. She slept on and off until four. Now she just wants a hamburger. And her own bed." Isabel gestures to the bags of food. "If there's a Whataburger® in there, you'll be her new favorite person."

Straightening my shoulders, I grin. "There might be. Along with some fried chicken and grits, two personal pizzas, and an order of queso with chips."

"Shit, Connor. Well, now you have to eat with us." Isabel wraps her hand around my right wrist—her fingers skating over a patch of skin where my nerves were damaged after two separate surgeries on my broken arm. I stifle my hiss. A little pain isn't going to stop me from enjoying her touch.

"All right, Mr. FBI Special Agent," Nurse Sheila says before we make it to the door. "I didn't kick you out of the ward, but that girl in there needs her rest."

"Veronica needs a distraction." Isabel pulls me closer, clinging to me like she's about to fall over. "Connor won't stay long. She can have a hamburger, right?"

Nurse Sheila shakes her head, a vaguely disapproving hum escaping her pursed lips. "She shouldn't have anything besides clear broth and Jell-O for twenty-four hours after surgery." A moment later, she rolls her eyes. "But I won't tell anyone if you don't. Just make sure she takes it easy. No more than *half* of what she *thinks* she can eat. If that stays down, after an hour, she can have more."

That's enough approval for Isabel, who doesn't look back. Just holds the door open and ushers me inside.

Isabel

Under normal circumstances, I'd never dream of introducing Veronica to a man before we've even had dinner. But this? It's about as far from normal as a situation can get.

I haven't slept. Haven't showered. I'm still wearing the little black dress, though I pulled on a pair of fuzzy socks, my old college fleece, and my Chucks when I got the call about Veronica.

I doubt I smell very good, and I *know* I look like shit. My cheeks heat when I realize I sobbed all over Connor's shirt then *sat in his lap* and kept crying. But he didn't even blink. Just held me and made me feel like everything might be okay again. Someday.

"Veronica? Still awake?" I ask as I peek around the curtain. She's sitting up—as much as she can with all the wires and monitors attached to her body—and fiddling with the edge of the blanket. "This is Connor. Connor Davis."

He sets the bags on the table stretching across the bed. "Pretty sure there's a hamburger, a bacon cheeseburger, and a chicken sandwich in that first bag. And fries."

My daughter manages a half smile. "Ketchup too?"

Connor arches his brows. "I ain't a monster. There's *extra* ketchup."

She shoots me a look normally reserved for things like double pepperoni and school holidays, then turns her focus back to Connor. "So. You're dating my mom."

He's digging through the bags, but stops to glance at me, his eyes full of questions, before he starts to arrange as much of the food as he can fit on the little table.

"Yes, he is," I say, stepping closer to him so I can rest my hand on his back. "You okay with that?"

"Sure." She only has eyes for the food, and I have to repeat Nurse Sheila's warning twice before she tells me she understands and unwraps a bacon cheeseburger. But with her left arm in a cast and sling, as soon as she picks it up, all the toppings fall out, and tears shimmer in her eyes.

"Want to know the trick?" Connor asks as he finds a chair in the corner of the room and places it next to mine. "Watch."

He takes another wrapped cheeseburger, then lays it upside down in his left palm. "Since you can't use the hand that's in a cast yet, you need a couple of fancy moves to keep everything inside the bun. Isabel? Can you put her burger back together and wrap it up again?"

I don't know what he's doing, but in under a minute, he's connected with my daughter in a way I can't. A way she desperately needs. So I do what he asks, shoving the pickles and tomatoes back inside the bun before folding the paper again.

"When I was where you were, lil' bit, my right arm was messed up. So see if you can mirror my movements, okay?"

"Yeah, okay," Veronica says. She's no longer crying, at least, and I'm mesmerized watching the two of them together. How Connor almost immediately knew what she was feeling *and* how to fix it.

"Take the first corner of the wrapper and peel it back, but *don't* do the same thing with the other corner."

"Why not?" She's wary, but interested. A deep scrape on her cheek has swollen to twice the size it was this morning, but it didn't need stitches—thank God. Unlike her ruptured spleen. I'd do anything to be able to kiss it and make it better, but that doesn't work anymore. What she needs now? Connor understands in a way I don't.

"Because if those pickles fall out again, I'm stealing them." He winks at her and proceeds to show her how to fold the wrapper into a strange little envelope. "There you go. It gets awkward when the burger's almost gone, but by then, you've eaten most of the good stuff anyway."

Veronica takes her first bite, and her smile? It's the most beautiful thing I've ever seen. "Go slow, baby girl. Nurse Sheila said you shouldn't have more than half of what you *think* you can eat. Just in case."

"Mom..."

There's the attitude I've missed. Maybe she *will* be okay. Eventually. "I mean it, Veronica. You were sedated less than twelve hours ago."

Shit. The haunted look is back in her eyes, and she returns her focus to the cheeseburger. Until Connor pulls out the container of queso. Then she's all about the chips.

I can't muster my usual enthusiasm for spicy melted cheese, but I manage a few bites. Until Connor rests his hand at the small of my back and starts rubbing small, slow circles over my tight muscles.

"I'm sorry I messed up your date," Veronica says quietly as she sets the remains of the cheeseburger on the table. "Mom was really excited."

Connor scoots his chair closer to the bed and leans forward with his elbows on his knees. "You didn't 'mess up' anything. This ain't the date either of us planned, but I couldn't ask for better company. Pretty sure your mom feels the same way."

My eyes burn, and I nod. If I try to speak, I'll burst into tears. Veronica's the most important person in my life and always will be. But Connor just won more points than I thought possible—just by talking to my daughter like she matters.

AFTER A HALF SERVING of chips and a bite of cheesy grits, Veronica falls asleep. Connor wraps his arm around my shoulders and presses a kiss to the top of my head. "I should go. Let you get some rest too."

"Have you ever tried sleeping in these chairs?" I shift, my back protesting the movement. "If she weren't being discharged tomorrow, I'd ask for a cot, but I can manage for one night."

Connor moves behind me, and his strong fingers dig into my shoulders.

"Oh, God. That feels amazing." Closing my eyes, I let his touch ease some of the tension I've carried since Leah's first phone call. "Where did you learn how to do that?"

"A lot of physical therapy."

His lips brush the shell of my ear, and goosebumps race down my arms. Our timing is horrible. I shouldn't be so attracted to this man with my daughter lying in a hospital bed two feet away. But my body doesn't seem to care.

All too soon, he stops, smoothing his hands halfway down

my back until he stops right above the band of my bra. "If you need *anything*, Isabel, promise you'll call me?"

I peer up at him, and his hazel eyes are dark with need. "I promise. And I won't disappear on you again. I'll text you when we get home tomorrow."

"Good." Shoving his hands into his pockets, he backs toward the door. "I'll make some calls about Mitzi. Can you send me her last name?"

"Nelson. Mitzi Nelson." I can't let him go without kissing him. I don't care that it's wildly inappropriate. I *like* this man, and I need him to know it. "I'll walk you out."

"I can find my way. Tell Veronica I'm glad I got to meet her." He's out the door in seconds, and I hurry after him, catching him halfway to the elevator.

"Connor, wait." Stepping in front of him, I screw up my courage and wrap my fingers around his biceps. "What you did for us... The food, helping Veronica, just...being here..."

"Ain't nothin' special, darlin'." His smile could melt the polar ice caps. And knowing what those lips feel like? After Veronica's healed—and I find some way to lock her in her room for the rest of her life—we're going on a proper date. One that doesn't have to end at the stupidly early hour of 9:00 p.m.

"It's special to me." I lever up on my toes and drape my arms around his neck. "*You're* special."

Connor tangles his fingers in my short hair, his gaze so intense, I want to look away, but can't. And then he kisses me. The heat of his mouth on mine? The way the hard muscles of his chest shift against me? My nipples tighten, and in this brief, perfect moment, all I want is him.

Until a scream pierces the din of the busy hospital.

"Veronica!" I jerk out of Connor's embrace and run. He matches my pace, and as we reach the door, alarms start blaring at the nurses' station.

A man dressed in a pair of green scrubs and a mask stands

over Veronica's bed, a syringe in his hand. She's fumbling for her IV with her left hand, but the cast foils her movements. My heart leaps into my throat. "Get away from her!"

The man slaps my daughter across the face, then tosses the syringe into the sharps container on the wall. Connor shoulders past me, spins the guy around, and drives an uppercut into his chin. The crack is so much louder than I expect, even with alarms going off all around us. Blood dribbles from the man's lips, and he snarls. "Fucking asshole."

"You ain't seen nothin' yet," Connor mutters and balls up his fists again.

But one of the nurses rushes in, then screams. The momentary distraction lets Veronica's attacker sweep his leg out to catch Connor in the knee. With a groan, he goes down, hard.

"Connor!"

He lunges, trying to grab the attacker's ankle, but the man's too quick and sprints out the door after shoving the nurse against the wall.

All I can think about is my daughter. She's dazed, but still trying to reach for the needle taped to the back of her hand. "M-mom...help..."

A second nurse barrels her way into the room. "Ms. Lopez, stand aside," one of them orders, but I know what my baby girl needs. That IV. Out of her. Right now.

I don't pause, don't warn her, don't even think about it. Just rip the needle out so quickly, blood splatters the blankets. "Get a doctor. Now!"

Scrubs guy put something in her IV. If I wasn't fast enough...

Yelling. Someone's yelling. Connor. I can't let go of Veronica's shaking hand, but I blink hard and try to focus.

"Call the police. Right fucking now," he roars.

"N-no..." Veronica slurs. "Mom, no. He can't..."

I don't know what's going on, but I know my daughter, and

even though she's obviously hurt, obviously been given *something*, she's still coherent. And very afraid. "Connor! No police!"

"Isabel—" He limps over to me, doing his best to keep out of the nurses' way. Veronica's heart rate is too low, and one of them calls for a doctor. "Someone tried to hurt her. I will *not* let them try again."

"Veronica said no." Sheila orders us to wait against the wall, but I can't move until Connor takes my arm. "She's smart," I say, peering up at him as he guides me to the corner of the room. "She has a reason."

"All right, darlin'. We'll wait. For now. But I'm stayin' right here."

Tears spill onto my cheeks, and when Connor wraps his arms around me, I let myself shatter into pieces.

CHAPTER EIGHT

Connor

THREE NURSES and two doctors hover around Veronica's bed trying to get her heart rate back to normal. She keeps falling asleep—or passing out—and no one knows what that asshole gave her.

"They're doing everything they can," I whisper for what feels like the hundredth time.

Every few minutes, Isabel tries to get to her daughter, but the doctors need room to work, so I hold her tight in my arms, even when she curses me and tells me I can't possibly understand what she's going through. My gaze keeps straying to the window in the door. There are too many fucking people passing by. The hospital needs to move Veronica to another room—one that doesn't have her name on it—and I need to make some calls. Get official protection for her. But I can't do that until I find out why she's terrified of the police.

After twenty minutes, one of the doctors pulls off his gloves and dumps them into the trash with a heavy sigh. "We can't be positive until we test her IV bag, but it's likely she was given a beta blocker. It's a drug that can lower your blood pressure and heart rate. Some epinephrine brought her vitals back in line, but we'll keep a close eye on her for the rest of the night. Expect one of the nurses to be in here every hour at the least, and if her heart rate drops below sixty, we'll have to administer another dose."

Isabel sags against me, a fresh trail of tears staining her cheeks. I'm not sure she could stand if her life depended on it. "She'll be okay?" she asks, her voice trembling.

"She should be. But we need to report what happened to the authorities."

Veronica starts to protest, but I meet her gaze and hold up my hand. "Dr...?"

"Dr. Wright. And you are?"

"Special Agent Connor Davis, FBI." Shifting to tuck Isabel under my left arm, I reach into my jacket pocket for my ID. "The Bureau will handle this case from here. I trust I don't have to sequester you and your staff until we can bring in additional security?"

The doc stares at my billfold with such intensity, I wonder how quickly I could get in touch with Brent this time of night. But just when I'm about to go on the offensive, he blows out a breath. "Fine. But the hospital is liable for the safety of our patients, and if you can't provide adequate protection for Ms. Lopez ASAP, I *will* call in Austin PD."

"Fair enough. How fast can y'all move her to another room?"

After a quick glance at the last remaining nurse fussing with Veronica's pulse-ox meter, Dr. Wright frowns. "It'll take at least half an hour. We can transfer her down to the eighth floor now that she's not critical. Into a shared room."

"Oh, *hell* no, doc. She gets her own room. A double so there's a bed for Isabel to get some sleep. And you'll station a security guard outside her door until I get a team in place. The only ones in or out of her room until further notice are you, one nurse you'll designate, her mother, and me. Got it?"

Isabel stares up at me like I've just given her the world, and when Dr. Wright reluctantly agrees, I jerk my head toward the door. "Give us the room until you're ready to move her, but if it's one *minute* over thirty, I'm talkin' to the hospital administrator, even if I have to get them out of bed to do it."

Once everyone leaves, I wedge one of the chairs under the door knob, then limp across the room to rest my back against the wall so I can keep an eye on the hallway. My knee throbs with each beat of my heart, and when I reach down to rub it, I have to stifle my hiss of pain. It's going to swell like a motherfucker before long.

Isabel squeezes onto the bed next to her daughter and Veronica starts to cry. "I'm so sorry, Mom. This is all my fault."

"Want to tell me why you're scared of the police?" I ask. Even though I keep my voice gentle, Veronica's whole body goes rigid. "No one's going to be angry with you, lil' bit. But whoever tried to kill you? I'd lay odds they're gonna try again."

She sniffles and pulls away from Isabel. "Mitzi didn't leave me at the library. W-we got in touch with Jamie. The woman at the sober living home who'd had her friends go missing?"

"Veronica! I told you to let the police handle the case," Isabel chides.

"I should have listened." Swiping at her cheek, Veronica tugs at the thin blanket. "Jamie agreed to meet with us, so we went down to the bus station on MLK. She said a man named Reggie Boswell had been calling her like ten times a day. Even after she blocked his number, he just started using a different one. Then he showed up at her job. She was so scared, Mom. He threatened to tell Child Protective Services that she was using again so she'd never get her kids back."

"Why would they believe this Reggie asshole?" I ask.

Isabel shoots me a look and mouths, *"Language."* Shit. I can't remember the last time I was around a kid for any length of time.

Veronica sniffles. "Because the police officer who was here earlier—Officer Milton?—he works with Reggie." Her voice fades, and I glance at her heart rate monitor. It's ticked up in the past couple of minutes, and if we're not careful, the nurse will be banging on the door.

"Baby girl, how do you know that?" With a gentle touch, Isabel brushes a lock of hair off of Veronica's forehead.

"Because Jamie told us she had to go. That she had to meet Reggie down at the abandoned strip mall on Orchard. We... followed her."

Veronica's heart rate shoots up from seventy-three to ninety, and I make it to the door just as the nurse tries to come in. Removing the chair, I block her access. "She's upset, but she's fine. Unless you're ready to move her, you're not coming in right now."

"Agent Davis, you are *not* in charge of my patient. Let me in or I'll have you removed from this hospital."

Her tone tells me she'll do it, and there's no fucking way I'm leaving Isabel and Veronica alone. "You have two minutes."

"I *have* as long as I need." With a huff, she shoulders past me. "Young lady, you need to stay calm. The epinephrine we gave you makes you more susceptible to a blood pressure spike, and that could be dangerous."

"I'm sorry," Veronica sobs and buries her face in the crook of Isabel's neck. If looks could kill, that nurse would be flat on the floor.

"Get out." Isabel points to the door. "You will *not* make my daughter feel guilty for having emotions." When we're alone again, she mutters, "Nurse Sheila was *a lot* nicer. Take a couple of deep breaths, V. I need you to tell us the rest of it, and I don't want that battle axe coming in again."

I don't bother with the chair this time. Just lean my entire body against the door. No one's getting in here unless they're a hell of a lot bigger—and more ornery—than I am.

After a minute and a couple of sips of water, Veronica continues. "We parked a couple of blocks from the old mall. Mitzi refused to go in, but I wanted to get proof Reggie was blackmailing Jamie. I told her to wait on the corner, and I snuck in. I got video and everything. Real, hard evidence, Mom. He hit Jamie in the face and Officer Milton was there pointing a gun at her. There was another guy there too, but he left, and I was about to..."

More sobs, and the kid's going to start hyperventilating if she doesn't calm down. "Veronica!" I say sharply. "Tell me five things you can see in this room. Right now."

"Huh?" Her dark brows furrow, but the question alone distracts her enough that her heart rate stops climbing.

"Five things you see. List 'em off."

"Mom, you, the TV, the water cup, and the whiteboard."

I nod. "Now four things you can feel."

"Mom's hand, the sheet, the pillow, and the blanket." After a shuddering breath, she sniffles and Isabel passes her a tissue. "I'm okay now."

"Not yet. Three things you can hear. Two things you can smell. One thing you can taste. Get through all of them. Okay and calm are two different things."

The relief on Isabel's face as Veronica lists everything I asked for and relaxes against the pillows is so damn heartbreaking. How she hasn't totally lost her shit is beyond me, but I suppose when you're a parent, you gotta find a way.

"Good job. If you start to feel panicky or have trouble breathing, go back to that, and try to pick different things every time. Got it?"

She nods carefully, tiny lines of pain bracketing her eyes. I remember my first couple days in the hospital. How every time I moved my head, it felt like the baseball bat was slamming into my skull over and over again. Swallowing hard, I clench my right hand behind my back. Isabel and Veronica don't need to know I'm barely holding on too.

"Go on, baby girl. You had video of the officer and Reggie threatening Jamie?" Isabel keeps her tone light, but I can hear the slight wobble, and I wish I could comfort her.

"There was no service inside the mall, so I couldn't upload the video. I was about to leave. Really, I was. But then I heard Mitzi scream."

Half an hour later, I follow behind an orderly moving Veronica to a room on the eighth floor. She and Isabel are exhausted, and thank God they aren't paying much attention to me. I can't hide my limp. The end of the hall is surrounded by a soft glow—one of my ocular phantoms making itself known—but it's manageable. For now. Only a little dizziness so far.

As soon as I know Isabel and Veronica are safe, I can call in reinforcements and send a dozen Texas Rangers to that abandoned mall to search for any sign of Mitzi. Every person we pass is a potential threat, but most pay us little to no mind.

In the elevator, Isabel leans against me, winding her arms around my waist. "I think she's asleep."

"Good. She's been through enough the past twenty-four hours. You have too, darlin'. As soon as she's settled, you should try to rest."

With a sigh, she shakes her head. "I can't. What if that man comes back? Or that cop?" There's so much fear in her eyes, my heart aches.

"I'll be right outside the door all night. No one's getting to Veronica again. I promise."

Isabel's about to protest when the elevator doors whisper

open and I tell the orderly to wait. "I need to check the hall first. Do not take one step out there until I do."

The man rolls his eyes, and I'd tell him to go fuck himself if there weren't a seventeen-year-old girl a foot away. Asleep or not. Veronica will be safe if I have to interrogate every single doctor, nurse, med tech, orderly, and janitor in this entire goddamn hospital tonight.

This floor is almost empty compared to the critical care unit, and in under ten minutes, she's secure in a private room with a keypad on the door and an empty bed for Isabel. Only the nurses' station, Isabel, and I know the code.

"I should call Leah," she says. "The police haven't told her anything—"

Guiding her over to the second bed, I pull back the blanket. "You can't, darlin'. If this Reggie dickwad finds out Veronica talked, he won't have any reason to keep Mitzi alive."

"Oh, God. No." Isabel fists my shirt with both hands. "Connor, Mitzi and Veronica are like sisters, and Leah's one of my only close friends. I can't keep this from her."

"You can." Holding her gaze, I lower my voice. "I'll take care of this, darlin'. Legally, the FBI doesn't have jurisdiction unless we know Mitzi's been taken across state lines, but the Ranger Division can investigate without involving Austin PD. In an hour, I'll have two Rangers outside this door and send someone I trust to take Leah into protective custody. By tomorrow, we'll have a safe house set up for y'all."

"A safe house?" Isabel sinks down onto the bed, her shoulders slumping and defeat swimming in her eyes. "We have to go home." She doesn't make a move to lie down, so I slide an arm under her knees and ease her legs up so I can remove her shoes.

"Home isn't a good idea right now." Pressing a kiss to her forehead, I wait for her to curl onto her side. "Get some sleep.

I'll be sittin' in that corner all night. When you wake up in the morning, we'll have a plan."

She's asleep before I can tuck the blanket around her, and I lean down to brush my lips to her forehead. Time to get to work. That chair ain't gonna do me any favors, but I can't sleep until I know Isabel and Veronica are protected.

CHAPTER NINE

Connor

I DON'T KNOW what possessed me to grab my Bluetooth earbuds when I left my apartment, but I offer up a quick thanks to the Universe for the assist. I don't want to wake Isabel or Veronica, but I need to call Brent and my contact with the Texas Ranger Division—AJ Stone.

After flashing my ID around all over Hell's half acre, Brent has to be first.

"Connor? It's after ten. What are you doin' callin' me this late?" His voice is raspy and thick, and I cringe when I realize I woke him up.

"Are you eighty? Don't tell me. You love those early bird specials and senior discounts."

"Fuck you. What's so important?" He's all business now, and a door closes in the background.

"You might get a call about me. Had to pull rank with Austin Mercy Hospital's staff to stop them from calling the police after an assault and attempted murder of one of their patients."

"Are you out of your damn mind? *Attempted murder?*"

Shit. *Think before you speak next time, idjit.*

I know that tone. He's pissed as hell, and if I'm not careful, I'll be the one behind bars. By the time I finish explaining the situation, he's calmer, but I need his word he'll let me handle this.

"Brent, I got two options. I can call my contact in the Ranger Division, but I'd feel a hell of a lot better if the Bureau could take this case."

Silence. This ain't good. Neither is the sigh that carries over the line. "Unless you know the missing girl was transported over state lines, we can't touch it. And even if she was, we're stretched so thin, I have agents working sixty- to seventy-hour weeks. The new guy—out of Atlanta—starts tomorrow, but even that's not enough."

If I thought it would do any good, I'd beg, but since I'm part of the reason Brent's in this position, I can't say a damn thing. "You know anything about the guy who helped find me? AJ Stone? He's a Captain with the Rangers."

"Nope. Other than readin' his name on the official reports. But he got pulled in because of that mercenary group out in Seattle connected to your brother, right? Ask *them* if he's trustworthy. I gotta get some sleep. Keep your ID in your fucking pocket for a while, will you?"

The call ends, and I'm left staring at my phone wondering why I didn't think to ask Quinton—or Graham, his guy—about AJ in the first place.

Because you're exhausted. And you never wanted to hear the details about your rescue.

It's early enough out in Seattle I don't worry about waking my brother with a quick text.

Can you ask Graham how much he trusts AJ Stone with the Texas Rangers? Got a case that can't involve the police. Need an answer quick if you can.

The electronic keypad beeps, and I'm up and out of my chair so fast, the room starts to spin and I have to brace my hand on the wall so I don't fall over.

"Hi hon," the nurse says as she slips through the door. "How's our patient?" She pauses, narrows her eyes at me, and frowns. "You look like death warmed over yourself."

"Post-concussion syndrome. Tryin' to stave off a migraine. I'm used to it. You don't have to wake Veronica up, do you?" Limping awkwardly after the nurse—her ID says her name is Rebecca—I try to loosen my tight muscles. Some protector I am. If I had to fight anyone right now, I'd probably topple over trying to throw a punch.

"Nope. Not this time. Just need to make sure all the machines are doin' their jobs." With a quick glance back at me, she adds, "I heard about you, Mr. FBI Agent. Makin' such a ruckus to keep her safe. You're one of the good ones, I think. If you give me ten minutes after I'm done here, I'll have a more comfortable chair brought in for you. The labor and delivery ward is across the atrium. They have recliners."

"Much obliged, ma'am. But what I could use more than anything? An ice pack for my knee. And it's Connor. Connor Davis."

"Got one of those too. I'll set you up, Connor Davis." With a smile, she turns her focus to Veronica, checking all the monitors and making notes on a small tablet. "Be back in two shakes with that ice pack, hon."

Nurse Rebecca leaves, and Veronica opens her eyes to meet my gaze. "Ice pack?"

"Got a bad knee. Nothin' for you to worry about," I say, steeling myself for the trip back to the uncomfortable chair.

The teenager darts a quick glance at Isabel, who didn't stir the whole time. "Is Mom okay?"

"She fell asleep the second her head hit the pillow. She's fine. Just tuckered out."

"I never should have left Mitzi," she whispers, tears gathering in her eyes. "What if they kill her? Or...*hurt* her. This is all my fault."

Leaning down and bracing my hand on the bed next to Veronica's shoulder, I keep my voice low. "If you hadn't run, they would have killed you both. Mitzi's alive because you escaped. They're not gonna kill her until they know you ain't gonna talk. She's their leverage. I know that's fucked—err, messed up—but you did the exact right thing."

"You'll find Mitzi? The FBI, I mean?"

Hope is a dangerous thing. Too much, and you're bound for disappointment. Too little, and you're hard pressed to keep fighting. Veronica needs a healthy dose of hope right now, and while I won't lie to her, I can't tell her the whole truth either.

"I'm workin' on that. We'll have a whole team out lookin' for her real soon. "

NURSE REBECCA WAS as good as her word, though decidedly *not* pleased when I insisted on rolling the reclining chair in myself. I wasn't gonna let the maintenance guy within ten feet of Veronica. But being able to put my leg up with an ice pack over my knee makes what I have to do next a hell of a lot easier.

My brother texted me the moment I sat down and confirmed my gut instinct about AJ was spot on.

Quinton: AJ Stone is one of the good guys. Graham says he and his brother are friends with Austin Pritchard. The former JSOC commander? Austin runs his own company now. A lot like Hidden Agenda, but more focused on protection than rescue. You want his number?

Want? No. Need? That's a definite yes. I have all his contact information in under a minute, but before I can call AJ, my brother sends one last message.

Quinton: You okay?

Life was easier when I could ignore questions like that. But keeping my brother at arm's length almost got both of us killed, so I thumb out as honest of a reply as I can muster.

Not entirely sure. Don't worry. I'm being safe. I'll call you in a few days and let you know what's going on.

The scowling emoji he sends back tells me if "a few days" is longer than forty-eight hours, I'm going to get an earful. From him *and* Graham.

I scroll through my contacts and bring up AJ's cell.

"You have some nerve, Connor," he snaps when the call connects. "I've been tryin' to get in touch with you for a month now."

"I'm an asshole. Tell me something I don't know."

AJ snorts. "Belle is chasing squirrels in her sleep."

The ice pack falls to the floor and I almost drop my phone. "Belle had better be a dog. Because if she's not, I don't think your relationship's gonna last."

His laugh is loud enough, I'm worried it'll wake Isabel or Veronica—even through my earbuds. "Y'know, if you'd bothered to return my calls, maybe you'd have met her by now and you'd know for sure. Because I ain't tellin'."

"Done fucking with me? A kid's life is at stake."

AJ clears his throat. "Sorry, man. What do you need?"

He listens as I recount everything Veronica told us earlier. "That dirty good-for-nothin' cop, Milton, had them both tied up in the abandoned mall down off the interstate. The kid managed to get free, grabbed her phone, and ran. But it wasn't with her things when she got to the hospital."

"And the car accident?" AJ asks.

"Unrelated. Some dude on his way home from work with a busted headlight. Didn't see her in time to stop. She was conscious for a few minutes and saw Boswell on the side of the highway. He was about to cross when another car stopped and the driver yelled that she was calling 9-1-1."

"Thank God for small miracles. So, what do you need from me? The Bureau has a hell of a lot more resources than we do."

I rub the back of my neck, trying to ease a fraction of the tension gathered there. *Just say it. Telling AJ won't make you feel any worse than you already do.*

"I'm on leave. Hell, it might be permanent. Too fucked up to pass medical. Plus, this isn't exactly within our jurisdiction. I need the Ranger Division to find Mitzi and arrange for protection for her mother, Veronica, and Isabel. Put away the dirty cop and whoever else is involved. And while you're at it, hunt down Reggie Boswell and lock him up for good."

"Is that all?" AJ huffs and Belle—who's most definitely a dog—yips in the background. "Let me make some calls. But you're gonna need help. The kind that don't mind breakin' a few rules."

***

Isabel

The scent of antiseptic confuses me until I open my eyes. In the bed next to mine, Veronica sips a plastic cup of orange juice and stares off into space. Across the room, Connor sprawls in a recliner that's clearly not made for a man of his size while tapping away on his phone.

He stayed. All night. Every time I woke up, he was there. Talking in hushed tones to God knows how many people.

I pad over to my daughter's bed and haul my tired body up next to her. "How are you feeling, baby girl?" Her hair's a mess, and the bruise on her cheek is four shades of purple.

"Mom, I hate it when you call me that," she whines, but

rests her head on my shoulder. "Breakfast will be here soon. I ordered egg sandwiches."

"Yum." I can't muster the energy to care about food, but my stomach obviously didn't get the message, because it growls so loudly, Connor jerks up with a groan. "You doing okay over there, stud?"

"Stud?" He runs a hand through his hair, winces, and checks his phone. "Thank fuck," he whispers, and I'd chide him for his language, but honestly? After what Veronica's been through, making a fuss about profanity? Completely useless.

"What is it?" I ask.

"Two Texas Rangers will be here in an hour. They'll take y'all to a safehouse. The guy I know there—AJ—agreed to investigate. He's already got a team at the abandoned mall looking for any sign of where they took Mitzi."

"Oh. That's right. You said something about a safehouse last night." I don't know why I thought we could go home. Of course we can't. Someone tried to *kill* my daughter. "How long do we have to stay there?"

Connor meets my gaze, his bloodshot eyes braced with exhaustion. "Until we know—without a doubt—everyone involved is...somewhere they can't get to Veronica ever again."

"And that would be?"

"You really want me to answer that?" he asks with a pointed look at Veronica who is suddenly very interested in our conversation.

There is no "somewhere." He means dead. Shit. Stop asking questions when you don't want to know the answers.

The lock beeps, and Connor's out of his chair and across the room before the door opens. "I'll take that. No need to come in, ma'am."

"Connor? She's just delivering breakfast..."

He limps back to Veronica's bed carrying a tray. "No one comes in unless I vet them first."

"Are you going to taste test all of her food too?" I snag one of the wrapped sandwiches, expecting him to laugh, but his lips don't even twitch.

"That wouldn't be effective for any slow-acting poisons," he mutters, but does take the plate marked *Patient* for himself. "You mind, lil' bit?"

She's already working on the wrapper for the last remaining sandwich, folding it the way Connor showed her last night. "Nope," she says, popping the p like always. I didn't know how much I needed to hear her act...*normal.*

My eyes burn, and I face the window rather than let my daughter see me break. The wannabe McMuffin tastes a lot like greasy cardboard, and I choke down the first bite, then set it back on the plate. I'd kill for a cup of coffee. Or tea. Really strong tea. With bourbon.

"What about school?" Veronica asks. "If we miss more than a week, Mrs. Chandler won't let us take the AP exam." Her voice breaks, and I turn back to find a single tear balanced on her lower lashes. "If Mitzi can't take the test, I won't either."

"I'll talk to Mrs. Chandler." I rest my hand over her wrist, only just noticing the slight reddish mark. A rope burn.

"They tied us up, but Mitzi got my hands free. That's when we heard Reggie and the police officer talking about 'getting rid of' us. I wanted to untie her, but Mitzi told me to run."

"Isabel?" Connor's deep voice helps ground me, and I shake my head.

"Sorry. Just tired. What did you say?"

He skirts the bed, his limp so much worse than usual, and I almost ask him what happened when it hits me. The guy who tried to kill Veronica kicked him. He never said a word.

"You need to eat, darlin'. You want somethin' else? Name it, and I'll make it happen."

He's so earnest, I believe him. If I wanted a lobster roll right now, he'd find the best seafood restaurant in Austin, track down the owner, and make them fire up the lobster pot.

I pick up the egg sandwich again and try another bite. It didn't get any better. "I'm fine. This safehouse will have a coffee pot, right?"

Connor chuckles. "Yes, ma'am. Coffee pots are standard equipment. Along with microwaves, stoves, refrigerators, and pizza delivery on speed dial."

"Pizza every night?" Veronica asks.

"No," Connor and I say in tandem.

It feels so good to laugh, I almost forget that my daughter has six stitches in her side. That her best friend is probably scared out of her mind. That more than one person wants them both dead.

"Pizza tonight. Something healthier tomorrow, deal?" I nudge her shoulder, hoping that when this is all over, the light will return to my baby girl's eyes.

CHAPTER TEN

Isabel

"WHAT DO you mean 'another four hours'?" Connor growls with his phone pressed to his ear. "They're ready to discharge her, and there is no fucking—*fudging*—way we're gonna just drive around the city while your cleaning crew stands around with their thumbs up their...err...noses."

"He knows we can hear him, right?" Veronica asks. "And that thumbs go up asses?" For all the energy she woke up with, she's wiped now and keeps nodding off.

"He knows. And he also knows you're seventeen." Tugging the blankets up to her chest and fluffing her pillow, I wait for her to fall asleep again before approaching Connor, who's just shoved his phone back into his pocket. "What's wrong?"

"One of AJ's guys didn't check his messages until a few minutes ago. The condo unit they use for protective assignments has been vacant for six months and someone left a carton of milk in the fridge." He combs his fingers through his hair, a few strands sticking up oddly—right over the dent in his skull. "So they have to bring in the crime scene cleaners."

"Oh, God. That doesn't sound good. Then again, that expired milk probably smells better than I do right now." I've been wearing this dress for more than forty-eight hours, and I think it could stand on its own.

"You're fine, darlin'. AJ should be here in a few minutes with some fresh clothes for you. And a double cappuccino. Extra foam." His fingers skim the back of my neck, and he pulls me in for a gentle, almost chaste kiss.

"You asked a captain in the Texas Rangers to bring me coffee?" My cheeks catch fire, and Connor's about to kiss me again when someone knocks, and we jerk apart.

"And there he is." Connor opens the door, and a man with dark brown hair and bright blue eyes enters the room with a shopping bag in one hand and a cardboard tray with two large coffee cups in the other. A leather messenger bag is slung over his shoulder, and the Texas Ranger star glints from under the lapel of his tweed jacket.

After looking us up and down, he shakes his head with a soft snort. "Guess I should've known when you threatened to kick my ass if I got her coffee order wrong."

"Quit actin' a damn fool." Connor hands me the shopping bag and one of the coffee cups. "AJ Stone, this is Isabel Lopez. Veronica's asleep, so keep your voice down."

"It's a pleasure, ma'am." Angling his head toward the door, he makes eye contact with two men standing in the hall, and they nod, then turn their backs to us, blocking the entire room from view. "Those two are Sergeant Ted Billings and Sergeant Isaac McGrath. They're on the day shift and will be with y'all until 9:00 p.m. I'm still workin' on the night crew."

The first sip of coffee sends a jolt all the way to my toes, but it's nothing compared to my shock when I dig through the bag. A tank top with a built-in bra, soft black pants, a crimson sweatshirt, socks, and a package of women's panties. All in my size. Along with a toiletry kit. "You got all this for me?"

AJ shrugs. "Connor told me how long you'd been here. Only time I held vigil by a hospital bed, I was fit to be thrown out with the trash on the second day." AJ's eyes hold no emotion, closed off and cold—despite all that ingrained Texas charm—but I think there's a good man under the gruff exterior.

"Thank you."

He nods, then shoots Connor a pointed look. One I can read from a mile away.

"I'm going to go clean up and change. Y'all can talk about whatever it is you don't want me to know." Leveling a finger at them, I add, "As long as you make sure Veronica *can't* hear you."

Guilt flashes in Connor's eyes, but he offers me a half smile. "We'll be quiet. I promise."

I plant a quick kiss on my daughter's forehead, pausing just long enough to make sure she's still asleep. The two men retreat to the far corner of the room by the window, heads bent together.

As I'm about to close the bathroom door, it hits me. Veronica doesn't have anything to wear out of here. Dropping the bag on the counter, I rejoin Connor and AJ, who stop talking the second they see me. "Veronica is going to need clothes before she's discharged. Everything she was wearing was destroyed when they had to operate. Except her shoes. But those..." I wrinkle my nose. "There's blood all over them."

Connor rests his hand on the small of my back, and the heat of his palm centers me. "Now that AJ's guys are here, I can go to your place and pick up whatever you need for the next few days. Just tell me where to look and I'll pack a bag for both of you."

Can I really let Connor dig through my underwear drawer? Are we *there* yet? And how can I possibly make a list of everything Veronica will need to feel comfortable in an unfamiliar place?

"You're absolutely certain she'll be safe here for a couple of hours?" I ask, my gaze pinging between the two men.

"If it'll make you feel better, ma'am, I'll stay in the room with her." AJ unbuttons his jacket, exposing a leather holster on a thick belt and giving the gray metal handle of the gun at his hip a gentle touch, like he's checking to make sure it's still where he left it. "No one's gettin' past Billings and McGrath, but I brought my tablet with me. I can run the investigation from here for a couple of hours."

I don't want to leave Veronica. Not for a second. But I believe AJ when he says she'll be safe. "Then I'm going with you," I say, meeting Connor's hazel eyes. "It'll be a lot easier than trying to make a list and realizing later I forgot half of what we needed."

"Fair enough, darlin'. As soon as you're ready, we'll head out. You all right makin' a stop at my apartment on the way? If not, I'll take care of that right now and come back for you."

"Your—?"

"AJ's not the only one I called last night," he says, keeping his voice low. "Got some help that's off the books, and if you're comfortable with me bein' around a little longer, I'm gonna stay at the safehouse with you tonight. Zephyr—she's part of the team I called—might have questions for you or Veronica, and it'd be a hell of a lot easier for me to get answers if I'm there."

Warmth gathers in my core, a totally inappropriate response when my daughter's sleeping three feet away. But I can't help it. Every minute, I half expect him to run away. We went from coffee and kisses to oh-my-God-this-woman-is-more-trouble-than-she's-worth in under twenty-four hours. Yet, he's still here. Doing all these sweet things like remembering my coffee order and guessing my clothing sizes.

"Isabel?" Connor asks. "Gonna need an answer, darlin'."

"You can stay. I...I'd...like that." If AJ weren't here, I'd kiss this amazing man who has his arm around me, but then I remember I haven't brushed my teeth in two days, and my cheeks catch fire. "I'm going to clean up now. I'll be ready to go in fifteen minutes." Fleeing to the bathroom, I shut myself inside, wondering how the hell I got so lucky to find Connor right when I needed him.

Connor

"What'd you think of Pritchard?" AJ asks. He leans against the window, giving the parking lot a quick scan before returning his attention to me.

"He's...somethin'. I've never met the man, and he was ready to fly out here until I told him I wouldn't hear of it. He has this new hacker on the payroll—Zephyr something or other—and she's working on getting the security footage from the eleventh floor. The asshole who tried to kill the kid was wearing scrubs and a mask, but I doubt he walked in that way."

"Have her check the cameras in the parking lot too. Guy had to get away somehow."

"This ain't my first rodeo." A flare of light in my periphery makes me wince. Staying up most of the night was all kinds of stupid, even though I'd do it again in a heartbeat. Thanks to the ice pack the nurse dropped off, my knee isn't quite the size of a softball, but it's close, and every step sends stabbing pains up to my ass. All I need is for this migraine to take hold and I'll be in a world of hurt.

AJ snorts. "Didn't say it was. But you're not firing on all cylinders either. Those bags under your eyes could fit enough horse shit for the whole corral."

"Now who's the asshole?" Despite my words, I know he's right, and I owe him big time for dropping everything to take this case. "Listen, I know this is a big fucking deal. Rearranging your whole division on a few hours' notice."

"Missing kid...missing *anyone* is worth it," he says quietly, turning to stare out the window again.

I don't know all the details, but his brother, Jasper, told me AJ's wife disappeared a spell ago. Went out for a run and was never seen again. In this bright, sterile room, the weight of his grief looks like it's about to crush him. "You ever need—"

"Don't." The edge to his voice warns me he's wound tighter than a guitar string, and I hold up my hands and take a step back. "Sorry," he mutters. "Been two years."

Awkward silence stretches between us, and I pull out my phone to text Zephyr, giving AJ the space he clearly needs.

Connor: Probably don't need to ask, but you're checking the parking lot cameras too, right?

She replies in seconds.

Zephyr: I will. Once I get past the hospital firewalls. HIPAA makes this a hell of a lot more difficult. It was easier to hack the Boston National Bank.

I apologize for the distraction and shove my phone into my back pocket just as Isabel emerges from the bathroom. Steam wafts from the doorway, carrying the scent of industrial soap along with it.

"A shower has *never* felt so good," she says, crumpling up the shopping bag and throwing it into the trash. "But if I were home right now, I'd burn that dress."

"That's a shame. You looked damn good in it." I wrap my arm around her waist and pull her against me.

"You should get your eyes checked. I could have gone trick-or-treating as a zombie. Or a goth witch, at least."

"I told you, Mom," Veronica calls from behind Isabel.

Isabel groans, and I angle a glance at her daughter. "Told her what?"

"That the dress was hot. She wanted to wear a *pantsuit.*"

After an eye roll, Veronica yawns. "I smell coffee. Why do I smell coffee? Is there coffee?"

Hiding the cup behind my back, I kick myself. I had no idea the kid would want any.

Isabel looks as guilty as I feel. Extricating herself from the crook of my arm, she eases a hip onto the bed and takes Veronica's hand. "The place Connor's taking us won't be ready for a few hours. Would it be okay with you if AJ—that's AJ in the corner—stayed here with you so I can go home and grab what we'll need for a few days?"

Her eyes widen, and she shakes her head. "They have my driver's license, Mom. What if they're waiting for you at home? I don't need any of my stuff. Really."

Isabel pales, all her excitement at getting Veronica the things a seventeen-year-old needs to feel comfortable and safe disappearing almost instantly. "Oh, God. I didn't think..."

"We'll go to my place first," I say. "Give Zephyr a chance to see if there are any traffic cameras with a view of your house." *And get my service weapon.*

"I have a doorbell camera. And a security system." Isabel scoots closer to Veronica, her arm around her daughter's shoulders. "I *think* I armed it when I left for the hospital."

I approach the bed, doing my best not to limp. Holding out my hand, I make a fist, my last finger extended. Veronica might be seventeen, but you're never too old for a pinky swear. "I promise I won't let anyone hurt your mom. If it's not one hundred percent safe, we'll hightail it back here faster than a sneeze through a screen door."

Veronica chews on her lip for a long moment, her brown eyes full of fear. "Promise?"

I nod at my hand, and when she curls her pinky around mine, I give it a squeeze. "Promise. Your mom matters to me, Veronica. Nothin' in my world is more important than makin' sure the two of you are safe."

CHAPTER ELEVEN

Connor

ISABEL DOESN'T SAY a word the entire drive to my apartment. Her hands folded in her lap, she stares out the window, the occasional slow, deep breath making her shoulders heave.

"Talk to me, darlin'. Are you worried about going home?"

"I'm worried about everything," she says as I pull into my parking spot and kill the engine. "How much tragedy can Veronica handle in her life? She remembers losing her dad. Remembers how *I* dealt with it—or didn't...for a while. If Mitzi doesn't survive, I don't know that she will either. Not as the sweet, smart, funny kid I tried to raise."

"She's strong, Isabel. Fuckin' hell, she got away. And Mitzi? That kid managed to untie Veronica *while* bound, and had the wherewithal to tell her to run. Those girls are amazing, and they'll survive. Mitzi's probably trying to Nancy Drew her way out of there right now."

Isabel's laugh—though weak—is reassuring as fuck, and she curls her fingers around her purse strap. "The two of them read every single one of those books as a kid. *Hardy Boys* too.

One Christmas, they both asked for magnifying glasses, and a month or so later, when I lost my wedding ring, they turned it into a mystery they just *had* to solve."

"Did they find it?" I'm not sure I want to know. When Isabel talks about her late husband, her gaze softens, a hint of longing in her voice. I can't compete with Tony. Not with Isabel and certainly not with Veronica. I don't want to. But is the woman across from me even ready for a serious relationship?

"Earth to Connor..." She touches my arm, and the sparks race along my skin. "They found it under my dresser in this knot in the floorboard. After interrogating me five separate times. When had I taken it off, what was my usual routine, where had I already looked and why..." She stares out the front windshield, purses her lips, and swallows so hard, I can hear it. "They were twelve. And when I told Veronica I couldn't put the ring back on, it broke her a little."

A piece of my heart cracks and bleeds for the anguish written all over Isabel's face. "How long had it been?"

"Four years. She didn't speak to me for days." A tear shimmers on her cheek in the late morning sun, and I reach over and capture it with my thumb.

"What do you need? Right now. Tell me and it's yours." My knuckles crack as I ball my hands into fists. I *hate* feeling this helpless. I care about this woman, and she's hurting.

"I'm fine." She sniffles, straightens her shoulders, and forces a smile. "We can go in. I want to see where you live."

We're not done with this conversation. Because the longer I spend with her, the more I think I might want a life with her, and I need to know if she feels the same.

***

"How long have you lived here?" Isabel asks after I flip both locks on the door and arm my security system.

"Three months. Why?" Dropping my keys on the counter, I open my fridge and pull out a carton of orange juice and a container of yogurt.

"Because this place looks like it could be on the apartment building's rental brochure. A recliner, a TV, coffee table...all of five books on the shelf, and absolutely no personal touches at all."

I shrug, even though she's right. "Transferred from the Dallas field office to Austin following my boss. I wasn't even out of the hospital when I asked him to put my paperwork in. We've been friends for years, and I thought...maybe it'd be easier to come back if I were still working for him. I couldn't pack a damn thing, so I hired movers. Almost all my shit's in storage somewhere."

Isabel's eyes soften, and the intensity of this *thing* between us grows until we both look away. "I didn't mean to pry..." she says softly.

Way to make her feel like shit. You weren't raised in a barn. Fix this.

I reach across the counter and link our fingers, giving hers a gentle squeeze. "You weren't pryin'. I'm not used to talking about myself, and that's on me. Let me make you something to eat. I have eggs, breakfast burritos, yogurt, and cereal. What'll it be?"

"I can't," she says. Pressing her free hand to her stomach, she shakes her head. "I *know* I should. But..."

"But nothin'. Other than the food I brought last night and—what?—two bites of that awful egg sandwich, have you eaten *anything* in the past two days?" I already know the answer. We had coffee Monday morning, and her cheeks weren't this hollow then. Even the new clothes hang off of her. Maybe I gave AJ the wrong sizes, but my gut says I didn't.

She stares down at her feet, and her whispered response is

so faint, I have to strain to hear it. "No. The nurses offered, but..."

"If nothin' I have sounds good, we'll stop anywhere you want on the way to your house." Hiding my limp is getting harder and harder, but I shuffle around the counter until we're close enough the heat of her seeps into my chest. "You tell me what you want—or what you think you can stomach—and I'll get it for you. I don't care what it is."

"Why are you doing this?" she asks. The look in her eyes? She's truly confused, and it kills me that someone putting her first makes her feel this way.

"Because I care about you, Isabel. I know we went from strangers to...somethin' more in one-half less than no time, but we've both been on this earth too long to fuck around with relationships that ain't worth spit. When this is all over, if you decide I'm not who you want, I'll walk away. But somethin' tells me you feel *it*—whatever this is between us—as strongly as I do. Or you will, once you can breathe again."

Isabel drapes her arms around my neck, her head tipped back and her lips parted. For the first time since I got to the hospital last night, her gaze holds something other than fear. Need. Desire. More?

Slanting my mouth over hers, I savor the way she melts against me. Her curves, largely hidden by the baggy sweatshirt and yoga pants, make me want more. So much more.

Her little moan is a balm to my damaged soul. Lightly, I trace the seam of her lips with my tongue. The heat between us explodes into a five-alarm fire, and if I thought she was ready for it, I'd carry her into my bedroom and strip her naked right now.

Instead, I capture her lower lip between my teeth, tugging gently until we part, both breathless. "I'd apologize, but..."

"Don't you dare." Isabel grabs my forearms to steady herself, then takes a step back. "I can't promise you anything,

Connor. Not tomorrow, not next week...hell, not even tonight. Veronica has to be my priority."

"I know, darlin'. I won't make you choose. Ever. She's your daughter, and I'd be a complete asshole if I didn't give you the space you needed. But that doesn't mean I'm gonna walk away. Not unless you tell me to."

For several long moments, she doesn't reply, and I swear my heart stops beating.

"No," she says softly. "I can't do this without you. Or...I don't want to."

Relief washes over me, sweeter than stolen honey, and I gesture to the kitchen. "Then what can I fix you for breakfast?"

***

Isabel

When Connor emerges from his bedroom, the scents of leather and spice—along with the sight of his tousled hair and freshly trimmed beard—draw me to him. I shouldn't notice how good he smells or want to feel his beard scrape against my cheek again. I *should* be spending every minute thinking—worrying— about Veronica. But before she disappeared, I was excited about our date. About the possibility of more. And now that my life has turned upside down, Connor's showing me what kind of man he really is.

The kind I could fall in love with.

I dry the cereal bowl and spoon, but I wasn't paying enough attention when he got them out, and as I'm opening the third cabinet door, he comes up behind me and eases the bowl from my hand. "You didn't have to clean up."

"I need to do something. Otherwise my brain won't stop playing the worst-case scenarios on a loop, and that's exhaust- ing." Hugging myself tightly, I head for his living room window.

The view isn't much—a small slice of greenbelt next to a basketball court—but any distraction is a good one right now.

"Heard from Zephyr just a few minutes ago," he says. "She wants to do a video call. You mind if I connect with her before we leave? AJ texted right before I got in the shower. He and Veronica are fine. She's kicking his ass in some game on his tablet. *Ticket to Ride?*"

Knowing my daughter feels up to playing a game—and playing to win—eases some of the tension in my shoulders, and I nod. "It's fine. Plus, I'm guessing Zephyr wouldn't want to talk if it weren't important."

Connor shrugs. "I have no idea. Never worked with her before."

"And that's supposed to reassure me?" He cringes, and I regret saying anything. Hell, maybe I should ask him to take the call in his bedroom. What if I lose it and start grilling this Zephyr woman about her qualifications? That won't help anyone.

His warmth as he sidles up behind me is reassuring, though not enough to stop my heart from beating like a bass drum. I lean against him, and the rumble of his voice sends goose-bumps racing down my arms. "She works for the man who's responsible for saving my life. Austin Pritchard used to run the Joint Special Operations Command—one of the highest-level military operations in the United States. He retired a little over a year ago. Does his own thing now."

"His own thing?"

Connor wraps his arm around me from behind, his fingers splaying over my stomach in a gesture that's so possessive, the "strong, independent woman" in me should hate it. Instead, it makes me feel safe. Like nothing in the world could ever hurt me.

"Yeah. Black ops shit. Protecting the innocent, taking on cases the authorities can't—or won't. The man knows people all over the world. Including AJ Stone and his brother, Jasper. They were the ones who found me."

"Found you?" I turn in his embrace. Lines of strain crinkle around his eyes, and a muscle in his jaw ticks.

"Long story. Or at least not one we have the time for right now. Bottom line? Austin's the reason I'm alive. And some of the guys he works with saved my brother. He wouldn't have hired Zephyr if she weren't the best at what she does—and trustworthy as fuck."

"Then call her," I say. "I don't know any of these people, but I trust *you*. I'm not sure why, since I've known you all of two weeks, but I do."

ON SCREEN, Zephyr runs her fingers through her teal hair. "Still working on the hospital's firewalls, but Isabel's home security system was a breeze to hack."

"That's not encouraging," I mutter from a stool next to Connor. He's leaning against his kitchen counter, the tablet propped up in front of us.

Zephyr cracks a smile. "There are only a couple of systems on the market today I *can't* hack. If you want to upgrade, I can hook you up."

"Assuming Veronica and I can ever go home again, I'll take you up on that."

The low rumble in Connor's chest startles me. Did he just...growl?

"You'll go home. These assholes won't be breathing free air much longer. Or any air." He grips the counter hard enough his knuckles turn white, and Zephyr rolls her eyes.

"You should come out to Boston one day, Connor. You'd fit right in. Overprotective, growly, handsome..."

"Who are you callin' handsome, luv?" a man asks, his Irish accent unmistakable. "Don't tell me I have competition."

"Go to work, Ronan. I'm talking to Q's brother." Zephyr leans back on the couch, tips her head up, and waits for a lean, wiry man with dark hair to bend down and kiss her. "Pick up some milk on the way home? I'm going to burn through the rest of the carton with all the tea today requires."

The man—Ronan—nods, then stares at Zephyr's computer. "I see the resemblance. You and Q have the same eyes. You doin' all right, Connor?"

"No. Not while Isabel's daughter is in danger. Can we get back to business?" Connor's frustration rolls off of him in waves, and I rub circles over his lower back until he blows out a breath. "Sorry, Ronan. Zephyr. It's been a long twenty-four hours."

"I work with the grumpiest arse on the planet," Ronan says with a chuckle. "But give Zephyr some credit, mate. She knows her shit."

A few seconds later, a door closes, and Zephyr takes a sip from the biggest mug I've ever seen. "Now that the testosterone fest is over, can we get back to business? Isabel's security system hasn't logged any events since she armed it early Wednesday morning. I also accessed her doorbell camera, and other than mail delivery, no one's come up the walk."

"What about traffic cameras?" Connor asks.

"There aren't any close enough to Isabel's house. Plus, even if there were...it'd take me at least two days to write a program that could analyze all the cars coming and going."

"Zephyr..."

"It's on the list. I only started working for Austin a month ago. Facial recognition? That's a breeze. Runs off of Hidden Agenda's servers in Seattle. But cross-referencing the make and model of thousands of cars over the last thirty-six hours? The code alone is challenging, but the amount of processing power it needs is *huge.* Give us another few weeks and we'll have it, but until then...not much I can do. Plus, the city needs to upgrade their cameras. Almost impossible to make out the plate numbers."

"So, is it safe? Or...?" My stomach twists itself into a knot, and I'm about to tell Connor we should just stop at the nearest Clothes Mart and grab a few things for Veronica rather than risk it.

"From what I can see," Zephyr says, "it's safe. And you have an overprotective FBI agent there who looks like he'd burn down the world for you. So..."

"We're going." Connor tells Zephyr to call when she gets into the hospital network, tucks his tablet into a protective case, and disappears into his bedroom for long enough, I venture down the short hallway to find him.

He's sitting on his bed, a pistol cradled in his hands, and a look of utter defeat in his eyes. I'm about to back away when he notices me and tucks the gun into a holster. "Sorry, darlin'. Been a while since I..."

Fear, regret, worry...so many emotions churn in his gaze, but he pushes to his feet, snaps the holster onto his belt, and pulls two extra magazines from a small safe hidden in the bottom of his nightstand.

"I'm not range certified anymore," he says, slamming the safe door. "But I'm still a better shot than most."

I stop him before he slings his duffel bag over his shoulder. "I trust you, Connor. Even if you don't trust yourself."

CHAPTER TWELVE

Connor

THE GLOCK 19 is heavy on my belt. Familiar and not. For years, it was a part of me, of my morning routine. The first week or two I was out of the hospital, I opened the safe every day before I remembered I didn't need to—even though the only way I made it from one room to the next was with a walker.

Didn't matter.

Who am I without my ID and gun? Connor Davis, civilian? I stifle my snort and hope Isabel doesn't notice. She's still nervous about going home, and I scan the road around us constantly, cataloging every car, tensing once or twice and backtracking a few blocks when one follows for longer than a single turn.

After the most convoluted route possible between my apartment and Isabel's house, I pull into the driveway of the modest Craftsman. Paint the color of a desert sunset, sky blue trim, and a welcoming, expansive porch greet us, but Isabel doesn't make a move to get out of my truck.

"You're sure?" she asks, her shoulders hunching up around her ears.

"No one followed us. Your front door's still closed." I ease myself out and round the front of the truck with as much control over my gait as I can muster. The knee brace feels like it's strangling the life out of my leg, but at least I'm not in danger of the joint buckling with every step.

I help Isabel down, my hands on her waist, and meet her gaze. "Get your keys, darlin'. You unlock the door, then stay behind me. I'm gonna clear the house before I let you out of my sight."

"Clear...oh, God. Like with that?" She nods toward my gun. "We can go..."

"Standard procedure. Probably unnecessary. But I won't take any chances with your safety." Dipping my head, I brush a quick kiss to her lips, and some of the tension in her body eases. She fishes her keys out of her purse, but her hand shakes the whole time. "Deep breaths."

"I trust you." The declaration is so quiet, I think she's trying to reassure herself as much as me, but she lets me lead her to the door.

I test the lock. Good. Still secure. She steps out of the way quickly once the door's open, and I sweep my gaze around the neatly kept living room. Clearing a space? One of those things you never forget how to do. It's ingrained in us at Quantico. Second nature. Almost as natural as breathing. The gun's solid weight in my hands reassures me, and despite the nerve damage in my right forearm, my grip doesn't waver.

Living room, dining room, kitchen, pantry, two bathrooms and all three bedrooms. Empty—and to my eyes—untouched. "Anything out of place?" I ask once I've holstered my weapon and we're standing in Veronica's room.

"No. Thank God."

"What about smells? Any new ones? Body odor, cologne, anything?"

She offers me a little smile. "No. Just you."

I chuckle. "Is that a good thing?" Never been self-conscious about my own scent before, but being around Isabel is an exercise in the unknown. One I'll gladly add to my daily routine if she'll let me.

"Yes." Her fingers skim down my arm, coming to rest on my wrist where she squeezes lightly before turning to Veronica's dresser. "The suitcases are in the garage on the shelf above the workbench. Can you grab the big green one for me?"

"Of course. Pack enough for at least four days. Any longer and we can come back."

Isabel starts pulling items out of the drawers, and once I retrieve the suitcase and set it on Veronica's bed, I offer to help, but really...what the hell am I going to do? I don't know what either of them need. So I head for the living room and sink down onto the dark blue couch to wait.

Photos stare back at me from the mantle. Veronica on a bike as a kid, her standing with Isabel and a man who looks so much like Veronica, he has to be her father. A strange sensation churns in my gut. It's not jealousy. Not exactly. More like regret. The three of them look happy. The perfect family. Isabel is mid-laugh, holding a four- or five-year-old Veronica while Tony stares at them with awe.

"How long have y'all lived here?" I ask when Isabel busies herself in the kitchen for a few minutes.

"Almost seven years. After Tony was killed, everything in our house reminded me of him. Veronica didn't want to move, but I was crying every day, and just..." she waves her hand, "needed a fresh start. Why?"

I join her at the counter and cover her hand with mine. "I don't know how to do this, darlin'. You had a whole life with a man you obviously loved who loved you back."

"I did." Her voice carries such warmth when she talks about her late husband, and there's that regret again. Rising like a creek in winter. "But...he's gone, Connor." Her eyes shimmer, but she smiles, a little sad and a little wistful. "He'll always be a part of me. Veronica has his sense of humor, his resilience, his determination, and his smile. Every year on his birthday, we watch old videos together so she doesn't forget him."

"I don't want you to ever think I'm tryin' to take his place. Especially now. If you don't want me stayin' with you at the safehouse, I won't. I'm not your husband. Hell, I don't even know if I'm your boyfriend. And I'm practically movin' in."

Her little gasp surprises me, as does her palm over my heart. "You're definitely *not* a boy, Connor. And I hate labels. I'm a 'widow' and a 'single mom' and a 'strong woman' and all these other *things* that don't tell people anything about who I really am. You're important to me. I care about you, and I want you in my life. Can that be what we are for now?"

Nodding, I pull her close, and Isabel rests her cheek against my chest. I can do "no labels." As long as I know she wants me, I can do anything.

<hr>

Isabel

I packed too much. Veronica's favorite blanket, her pillow, and more than a dozen loose sweaters and t-shirts to accommodate her cast and stitches. "Can we fit this too?" I ask, holding up the stuffed whale Tony bought her when she was seven.

"We can fit anything you need, darlin'," Connor says from the kitchen. He cleaned out the refrigerator while I packed—something that didn't even occur to me—and now he's wiping down my countertops.

For several long moments, I stare into the whale's faded

eyes. If anything happened to the plush animal, Veronica would be heartbroken, so I slide him back onto the shelf above her bed. "Watch over the place, Sasha." With a final pat to her tail, I zip up the suitcase and roll it out to the living room. "I think this is it."

"Not quite." Connor joins me and holds out his hand. "I need your phone."

"My phone? It's been dead since last night. Why?" Wrapping my arms around myself tightly, the suitcase between us, I peer up at him, completely baffled.

"It stays here. Along with anything else that has a GPS chip. I doubt Boswell has the skills—or the brains—to run a trace, but the cops could." He motions for me to hand it over, and the sweet, understanding man who emptied my fridge is gone. This is Connor Davis, FBI Special Agent. The change in his demeanor is both reassuring and terrifying.

Digging in my purse, I pull out the phone. "What about work? I'll have to call my office soon. I told them I had a family emergency, but that won't be enough for them for long. And Veronica's school..."

His gaze softens, and he sidesteps the suitcase to take me in his arms. "I'll pick up a couple of burner phones tomorrow. No GPS in older models. You can call anyone you want as long as you don't tell them where you are or any details about Veronica's...situation."

"Okay." I don't know why the idea of giving up the hunk of glass and plastic is so unsettling. It ran out of juice not long after Connor got to the hospital, and I didn't bother to plug it in. Why? There wasn't anyone I needed—or wanted—to talk to. Still isn't, besides the man in front of me and my daughter.

Pull off the Band-Aid, Isabel. Don't think about it. Just...let it go.

When I do, Connor checks to make sure it really is dead, then sets it on the coffee table. "I'm sorry, darlin'. I know this is a lot." He leans down and brushes his lips to mine, but before I can wrap my arms around him, his own mobile buzzes in his pocket.

"Son of a bitch," he growls when he checks the screen. "Leah Nelson is two minutes away."

"Wh-what? I thought you said she'd be in protective custody?"

"She was. Still *is*, technically. One of the Rangers assigned to her just texted me." He rolls his eyes, and his fingers fly over the tiny keyboard on his phone. "She went out the bathroom window, found some civilian on the street, and begged him to use his phone to call a cab. By the time her detail caught sight of her, she was gettin' in the taxi."

With a quick glance at the front door, I swallow hard. What am I going to say to her?

I'm sorry.

I wanted to call you.

Connor says there's every reason to believe Mitzi's still alive.

I can't say any of those things.

"Can I...talk to her?" No lie, I almost hope Connor says no.

"If you don't, I'm worried she'll cause a scene as big as hell and half of Texas." He rubs the back of his neck with a groan. "Invite her in. But let me do most of the talking."

Brakes squeal outside, and a moment later, Leah bangs on the door so hard, it shakes. "Isabel! Open up right now!"

The sun glares off the taxi cab window as it pulls away from the curb, and before I can ask Leah to come in, she slaps me so hard across the face, my whole cheek stings.

"How could you?" she screams.

"Fuckin' hell." Connor's boots echo on the hardwood floor as he rushes over to me and wraps his arm around my waist. "Touch her again, and I'll have you locked in a windowless room with a bucket rather than the cushy apartment you just escaped from. Get in here before the whole neighborhood hears your hollering."

Leah stalks past us in silence, and after Connor slams the door, he cups my chin and angles my head to examine my cheek. "That's gonna swell. Don't get within arm's reach of her again. I'll get you an ice pack."

I want to tell him not to bother. That I deserve a little pain. My child is safe. Protected. And hers isn't. But Connor's already rummaging in my freezer. "Leah, I'm sorry—"

"You're a piece of work, you know that?" She paces back and forth in front of the mantle, her hands balled into fists at her sides. "Veronica turns up—without Mitzi—and you don't even contact me? Maybe if you hadn't been such a complete and total bitch, Mitzi wouldn't be out there scared and alone, in the hands of some...some..."

"Someone who knows Mitzi is much more valuable to him alive and unharmed," Connor says as he hands me a bag of frozen corn. "If you want to be angry with someone, Ms. Nelson, I'm right here. *I'm* the one who told Isabel not to call you. I'm also the one who arranged for that protective detail keeping you safe."

She gapes at him, tears gathering in her eyes, and I drop the makeshift ice pack so I can hug her. "Leah, I wanted to call you. But Veronica was so scared when she woke up in the hospital. She didn't tell me anything until someone came into her room last night and tried to *kill her*."

Leah crumbles in my arms, sobs shaking her entire body. "I just want my daughter back," she mumbles against my shoulder. "I need Mitzi."

"I know, hon. I know."

"We're back," I announce after Connor punches in the code to Veronica's hospital room. "And we brought you something."

"Coffee!" Veronica squeals.

AJ yawns from where he's sitting at the foot of Veronica's bed. "Don't suppose there's one of those for me?"

"I'm not that much of an ass—*jerk*," Connor says and hands the Texas Ranger a tall cup of black coffee. "Cream and sugar packets are in the bag. Along with a couple of scones and some chocolate monstrosity that, apparently, Veronica would kill for, so I wouldn't touch it if I were you."

"You got me a choco-croissant? I love you, Mom."

It's so good to see her happy, even though the weight of our current situation—and Mitzi's—is evident in her gaze. Scattering flakes of pastry all over her hospital gown, she devours the entire thing—along with a sixteen-ounce macchiato complete with whipped cream. So much for the nurse's orders to keep things "light." I don't care. The color is back in her cheeks, and while she winces in pain more than once as I help her get dressed, when she's ready to go, she hugs me tight.

"Is Mitzi's mom okay?" she asks quietly. We're alone in the room, Connor and AJ waiting outside with the day shift Rangers, and I expect her discharge paperwork any minute now. "AJ said they found Mitzi's car and a few drops of blood in the old mall, but no sign of her."

Connor gave me the same update when I was almost done packing. "Leah...she came to the house." I touch my cheek gingerly. The skin is hot, but I covered the burgeoning redness with some foundation before we left the house. "She's scared, but she has two of AJ's guys with her, so she'll be safe."

"Can I call her? Please?"

"No, baby girl. I don't think that's a good idea." Smoothing Veronica's hair, I press a kiss to her temple. "Leah's hurting right now. Let's give her a little space, okay?"

Tears shimmer in my daughter's eyes. "She blames me, doesn't she? "

"No." After a beat, I let out a heavy sigh. "I honestly don't know, V. But if she does, she's wrong. You and Mitzi didn't cause any of this. The bad guys did."

"I wish I'd never signed up for the student newspaper," Veronica says, her tears finally spilling over. "If I'd picked chess club, we'd be at home right now."

"You hate chess, remember?" I lean in and rest my forehead against hers. "When I was your age, I had no idea what I wanted to do with my life. But you've known since you were twelve. You're an amazing journalist already, and you're going to get even better at U of A. This is who you are, and I'm so proud of you."

"Arm around my neck," Connor says. "Leave the crutch for your mom."

Veronica stares up at the five-story apartment building. "Isn't there an elevator?"

"No. Apparently no one in the Rangers ever blew out their knee. Or broke an ankle." Connor carries Veronica up two flights of stairs, his gait increasingly uneven. Shit. I keep forgetting he's injured too.

With a broken wrist, Veronica can only use a single crutch, but the brace that spans almost two thirds of her leg is so strong, she was able to do a couple of laps around the hospital room before she was discharged.

Sergeant Billings carries our suitcase with Sergeant McGrath keeping an eye on our surroundings. Every time I look back at him, he's staring out at the street, the parking lot, or up and down the stairwell.

When we reach Unit 322, Connor sets Veronica on her feet

and unlocks the door. "Go on in and pick your bedroom," he says when she has her crutch firmly under her right arm.

"She doesn't have to wait for you to...clear the apartment?" I ask, stopping my daughter from taking a single step until I get an answer.

Connor pulls out his phone, taps the screen a couple of times, and shows me an outline of what I assume is Unit 322. Every wall, window, and door—other than the front door—is green. "Motion and heat sensors in every room. Any movement or elevation in the ambient temperature will register on the app."

"Wow." As soon as Veronica crosses the threshold, the living room turns orange. This...could work. We might actually be safe here until AJ, Connor, and their respective teams find the men who hurt my daughter.

CHAPTER THIRTEEN

Connor

WRAPPING the leftover pizza in foil, I steal glances down the hall. Isabel and Veronica disappeared into the larger of the two bedrooms a few minutes ago. The kid almost nodded off into her last slice, and Isabel wasn't doing much better.

Billings and McGrath play cards in an alcove off the living room, and their replacements, Hardison and Elmore, should be here in a few minutes.

In the smaller bedroom, I set my gun and holster in the nightstand drawer and my boots next to the bed. For the tenth time, I wonder if I should move to the couch, but Isabel said she was going to sleep in Veronica's room tonight, and my whole body aches from so long in the hospital's shitty recliner. Tomorrow, I should leave. Go home. Let AJ's unit handle the case from here on out. But tonight? Tonight I'll stay close to the woman I'm falling for. Even if only to sleep.

Billings raps on the door jamb as I'm retrieving my tooth brush from my duffel. "We're headed out. Hardison and Elmore are set up out front. They've pulled overnights before, so y'all shouldn't hear a peep out of them. Elmore's teachin' Hardison ASL."

With a chuckle, I dig around for the toothpaste. "Handy skill to have. I learned a little at the Bureau."

"You ought to go meet Elmore, then. She'd be happy as a pig in shit to have you show Hardison how it's done. We'll be back in the mornin'. Captain Stone gets updates every four hours, so anythin' happens, he'll be here in a New York minute."

"I thought he lived out in bumfuck somewhere?"

Billings sobers and shakes his head. "He does. Damn fool keeps an apartment in town he uses Monday through Thursday nights. Goes home on the weekends. I reckon the ranch has too many memories for him day to day. But he won't give it up." With a final frown, the man says his farewell.

My phone buzzes when he and McGrath leave, and the exterior sensors on the doors and windows flash orange, then green. Locked up tight. Two red blips in the alcove, two in Veronica's room, and one in mine. Whoever set up this system is fucking brilliant, and I make a mental note to tell Zephyr about it when I talk to her. The last update I got wasn't good. She still hadn't managed to breach the hospital's firewalls, and from the number of four-letter words in her text message, she's pissed as hell about it.

Stretching out in bed after brushing my teeth, I stare at the ceiling. As exhausted as I am, I should have been asleep in seconds. Not wondering how Isabel's doing. Not wracking my brain for anything I didn't already tell Zephyr and AJ about the man who tried to kill Veronica. Not hoping that when this is all over, I'll have a chance to woo the strong, funny, beautiful woman on the other side of the wall. And maybe, find the family I never knew I wanted.

THE THUD and pained cry from the next room have me out of bed in an instant. "Isabel?" I don't think. Just race to their door and knock—hard. "Open up, darlin'. I need to know you're okay."

Elmore—a petite blond with fire in her blue eyes—rushes into the hall, her hand resting on her holstered weapon.

As I reach for the knob, Isabel opens the door. "We're fine," she says, her chest heaving in a purple tank that molds to her breasts in a way I shouldn't notice. And then I meet her gaze and see the bright red mark on her jaw. "What happened?" I drag a knuckle just under the subtle swelling, and she shies away from my touch.

"Veronica couldn't get comfortable. And, well..." Isabel huffs. "Cast meet face."

"I'm so sorry, Mom," the teen says. She sits up in bed and tugs at her Ruth Bader Ginsburg t-shirt. "I forgot you were right next to me."

"I know, baby girl. It's fine. But I'll sleep on the couch the rest of the night. I know that's what you wanted anyway." Isabel offers her daughter a smile. "No more smothering until the morning."

"I didn't do it on purpose." Hunching her shoulders, Veronica adds, "This bed just isn't...mine. And I want to bend my leg. It's driving me crazy."

"Dig your fingers into your upper thigh." I meet Veronica's gaze, and her eyes widen. Shit. I'm not wearing a shirt. Just my boxer shorts. Taking a step to the side so at least *some* of me is hidden by Isabel's body, I add, "On the outside of your leg. As hard as you can. It'll help."

"Cool." She starts poking under the blankets and when she finds the right spot, the relief on her face is obvious. "You should be a physical therapist, dude."

I chuckle and shake my head. "I'm not that sadistic. My PT

made me cry once or twice. Reckon he was trained by the devil himself."

From behind me, Elmore clears her throat. "I'm gonna make a pot of coffee and go back to teaching Hardison how to swear in sign language. He's determined to master at least a dozen of the more...*colorful* phrases by morning."

Veronica's eyes light up. "I want to learn—"

"You need to sleep," Isabel says. "And if I don't let you swear with your voice, what makes you think I'll let you do so with your hands?" She stalks over to the suitcase lying open on the floor, rummages inside, and comes back with a pair of thick socks and a sweatshirt before leaning down and pressing a kiss to Veronica's forehead. "Get some rest, baby girl. And enjoy having the bed all to yourself."

"'Night, Mom. I'm really sorry."

After Isabel steps into the hall and shuts the door, I offer her my hand. "You're not sleeping on the couch, darlin'. Come with me. You're takin' the bed. I'll be fine in the living room."

She tries to pull away, but I hold tight until she glares at me with what I can only describe as the "perfect mom stare."

"Connor, you were up all night in the hospital. I caught at least a few hours off and on. I will *not* take your bed."

"It's not my bed. It's yours. I'm only here until the morning. The couch'll be just fine." Leading her into the second bedroom, I pull back the blankets and stare down at her until she sighs and tosses the sweatshirt and socks next to the pillow.

"Fine. I'll sleep in the bed. On one condition." Hands on her hips, she challenges me with a wicked smile. "We share it."

My mouth opens and closes like I'm a fish out of water, and my boxers are suddenly tight enough, my dick starts to ache. "Don't get me wrong, darlin'. Ain't much I want more than you in my bed. But—"

"We'll keep the door open," she says. "I need to be able to

hear Veronica. But we're adults, Connor. We can sleep in the same bed without...foolin' around."

Swallowing hard, I angle my body in such a way I *hope* she can't see how aroused I am. Though from the way her nipples pebble under that tank...

Stop it. She's probably just cold. And you're an ass for staring at her chest.

It takes everything I have to force my gaze upwards, but the sight of her jaw swelling jerks me back to reality. "Yes, ma'am. But I'm getting you an ice pack for that bruise first." I should have done that five minutes ago, and now, I need the brief separation to calm the fuck down. She'll put a stop to this right quick if my dick gets much harder and all I want is to be close to her—all night.

When I come back, she's sitting with her back against the plain wooden headboard, rubbing her jaw gently. "She got me good."

Easing onto the bed next to her, I touch the cold pack to the bruise, using my other hand to hold her head still. The position has us face to face, close enough I can smell the hospital soap and something else. A light floral scent I could live in.

"The first few days with a cast, you bang it on everything," I say quietly. "Hurts like hell too."

"What happened to you?" she asks. I look away, and she takes over holding the ice pack, wriggling under the covers. "I know you were injured. But you never said how. Turn off the light and lie down. But tell me. Please?"

I'd relive the beating a thousand times if she asked me to, so I flick the switch and stretch out on my side facing her. With the light from the hall, I can still see her watching me, and I blow out a long, deep breath. "My brother's ex was crazier than...well, let's just say he's a couple of sandwiches shy of a picnic. Quinton tried to tell me, but I didn't see it. Couple of years ago, he fell down the stairs. His ex's fault. Alec—the sombitch—started drugging him after that. Kept him locked away in a condo downtown and had him convinced he'd suffered permanent brain damage in the fall."

"Oh, God. Some people really are evil," Isabel whispers.

"Damn straight." My knee starts throbbing in this position, so I roll onto my back. "I think I told you I broke his door and punched him to get Quinton out of there?"

"Still wish I could have seen that." Her laugh shakes the mattress slightly, and I wonder if I could ever get used to this—to pillow talk. For Isabel? I think I could do anything.

"Quinton was so fucked up—mentally and physically—he needed professional help. I got him into a facility, helped him change his name, move out to Seattle, start over. And then, I did somethin' so low, I had to look up to see hell."

Isabel scoots closer and rests her hand on my chest, right over my heart. "I doubt that."

"I left him. Went back to work—barely talked to him for over a year. Not until Alec started sendin' mail to his place in Seattle."

Neither of us say a word, and the silence is a physical weight pinning me down, clogging my throat and stopping my lungs from expanding. If I could take it all back—what I did to Quinton *and* what I just admitted to Isabel, I would. Take it back and hightail it out of here like my ass is on fire. But I can't, and after I touch my fingers to the permanent divot in my skull from that damn baseball bat, I find the strength to breathe again.

"I set surveillance on the asshole. But when I showed up to relieve them, he was gone. I was spittin' mad. And alone. Not watchin' my back. Alec had friends. They got the drop on me and I woke up half naked in Flash Flood Alley with a storm rollin' in and the two shitheads standin' over me with baseball bats."

Isabel draws in a sharp breath, and I can't tell her the rest.

Not in any detail. She's too raw. Too worried about Veronica and Mitzi to hear it.

"I'm only alive because my brother had started dating a member of a mercenary group out in Seattle. The guy got in touch with Austin Pritchard—Zephyr's boss—and he called in AJ and his brother Jasper."

"And your injuries?" Isabel asks. Shit. Her lips are so close to my ear, her breath tickles my neck.

"Concussion, fractured skull, separated shoulder, shattered kneecap, three breaks in my right arm, couple of fingers, more than one rib, nerve damage—"

Her kiss stops me, one arm draping over my torso, and she molds her body to mine. "You're the most amazing man I've ever met, Connor. To survive all that and be...who you are? Makes me feel like...Veronica might be okay too. Someday."

Cupping her ass, I pull her closer, her curves so fucking hot I may never fall asleep tonight. I'll just replay this moment— imagining what she looks like under that tank top and shorts— on repeat until the sun comes up.

Her skin flushes hot, but she doesn't make a move to retreat. Hip to hip now, I can't hide how much I want her. How hard I am for her. If we don't stop soon, we'll both regret it, and though my balls are gonna ache for hours, I break off the kiss. "Promise me something?" I ask, almost panting with need.

"Anything." Her voice cracks, and I think she's as turned on as I am.

"When this is all over, we'll do that again. Only we won't stop."

Isabel flops onto her back, and the absence of her heat, of her soft curves, leaves me cold until she links her fingers with mine. "Promise."

CHAPTER FOURTEEN

Isabel

THE SCENT of coffee tries to pull me from a dream I don't want to end. Connor's hands slide over my body, his thumbs hooking in my panties and dragging them down my hips. He groans my name inches from the apex of my thighs, but just as he's about to taste me, the mattress depresses, and the moment shatters into reality. A reality where my jaw and cheek ache, my eyes are dry as the heart of a haystack, and all I want to do is hide under the blankets all day.

"Mornin', darlin'." Connor's deep voice does what the motion and the aroma of coffee couldn't, and I open my eyes. "It's not a cappuccino, but it's strong and hot."

Like you.

Despite my exhaustion, I manage not to say the words aloud. His black t-shirt stretches across his sculpted chest and he's smiling, but when he hands me the cup, his right arm trembles slightly. I reach out and trace the thick scars running from just above his wrist to his elbow.

"Does it still hurt?" I ask.

"Here and there. Nerve damage. My fingers go numb sometimes." He shrugs. "Veronica's break was simpler. Three months, it'll be like nothing ever happened. Physically, anyway."

"That's not why I asked." Heat crawls up my cheeks, and I take a sip of coffee so I have a moment to figure out how to tell Connor I care about him. "I want to *know* you," I say, finally. "Last night..."

He leans down, cups the back of my neck, and kisses me. Before he draws back, he whispers against my lips, "Last night, I shared a part of me no one ever sees. Wouldn't have done that for anyone but you."

"That might be the most romantic thing a man has ever said to me." Connor's surprised laugh has me reaching for his hand. "I mean it."

"Wasn't meant to be romantic. Just the truth." He tries to get up, but his knee cracks, and he stumbles until his shoulder hits the wall. "Fuck."

"Connor!" I'm on my feet in an instant, coffee sloshing over the rim of my cup. With my free hand tight on his hip, I try to steady him. "How bad is it?"

"No worse than any other day, darlin'. Tripped on the edge of the rug." His voice takes on a rough edge that's so damn sexy, it sends goosebumps racing down my arms. "I'm not a good bet, Isabel. You deserve a man who's not broken. Who isn't permanently *disabled,* who can still do his job, still provide."

"Horseshit." I set the mug on the nightstand and tug on Connor's arm until he turns to face me. "I don't need someone to *provide* for me. I need someone to love me."

He flinches at the word love, and I think he's about to rush off when the rhythmic *clicking* of Veronica's crutch draws closer.

"Mom? Is there breakfast?"

Connor heads for the door, leaving me with my nipples hard and aching under my tank top. "We've got eggs and bacon, plus all the ingredients for pancakes and french toast too. Any of that sound good?"

"Pancakes," she replies, and the walls I built around my heart so many years ago start to crumble. He talks to her—cares for her—like it's second nature, and she's accepted his presence like she knows I don't ever want him to leave.

"Well, come with me, then," he says. "Let's see if we can have breakfast ready to go by the time your mom gets dressed."

When I turn around, Connor's following Veronica down the hall, his hand hovering just under her elbow, making sure she doesn't fall.

Broken, my ass. He's not broken. He's perfect.

BY THE TIME the dishes are done and both Veronica and I have bathed and dressed, Connor has his duffel packed and slung over his shoulder as he emerges from the bedroom.

"You're leaving?" I don't know what I'm supposed to do here all day—or what Veronica is going to do other than rest. Connor—along with Sergeant Billings and Sergeant McGrath —warned us we can't check our email, call any friends or family, or leave the safe house for any reason. Hell, my laptop is still at the office and I left Veronica's tablet at home. There aren't any books on the shelves here, but the TV has Netflix. Movie marathon?

"I'm gonna meet AJ. See about the investigation." He shoves his right hand into the back pocket of his Wranglers, small lines tightening around his eyes. "But I'll come back with dinner. What sounds good, lil' bit? Whataburger® or BBQ?"

On the couch, Veronica scrolls through an endless list of movies. She's propped her arm up with a pillow, and rests her braced leg on the coffee table. "BBQ would be awesome. Mom? Can you call Mrs. Chandler?" she asks, tipping her head back to meet my gaze. "Or the principal? I need to find out what I'm missing at school. And maybe...get Mitzi's assignments too? I could do them for her."

She's so desperate to help her best friend, and I'd give her anything she wanted if I thought it would ease some of the guilt she's carrying. But I can't give her this.

"We can't, baby girl. No phone calls, remember? I need to let my boss know I won't be in for a while too."

Connor limps back over to the couch and drops to his good knee in front of my daughter. "Listen, lil' bit. You're less than a year away from bein' an adult, and once that happens, no one's gonna let you lie on the couch all day watchin' Netflix. Take advantage of it for a few hours, and when I come back, I'll bring a couple of burner phones. Your mom can call her work and your school and figure out what we need to do so you don't fall behind. Deal?"

She nods, though I think she'd be a heck of a lot happier if he'd offered to drive her to school and leave her there all day.

I'm fixated on one word.

We.

"...figure out what we need to do..."

That implies he's accepted there *is* a we. I follow him to the door, and he wraps his arms around me and buries his face against my neck. "No going outside, remember? Do everything Billings and McGrath tell you. And rest. You hear me?"

"We'll rest. As long as I know you're coming back. And not *just* for dinner."

Connor straightens, and when our gazes collide, the uncertainty in his eyes? Shit.

He's not ready to "play house," Isabel. And you shouldn't be either.

But I am. Maybe it's our situation. Maybe I'm clinging to him because he's been the only constant in my life since he showed up at the hospital Wednesday night. Or maybe it's more.

"If I stay," he says, his voice raspy, "I'm gonna be hard pressed to ever leave you, darlin'. This...feels damn close to puttin' a label on us, and I won't do that if you're not ready."

I reach up to cup his cheek, dragging my thumb over his close-cropped beard. "I don't know if I can slap a label on what we have, Connor. If I'll *ever* be ready to do that. But that doesn't change how I feel about you. I want you in my life—in *our* lives. I want to wake up with you tomorrow morning. And the morning after that. And the one after that. If that means labeling us as 'official' or 'a couple' or 'boyfriend and girlfriend—'" I cringe, and the corners of his mouth twitch slightly, "—then so be it. As long as we're together."

His chest heaves as he takes a single deep breath, then drops his head so he can kiss me. It's not a peck. Not a quick brush of his lips. No. This is a deep, searing, all-consuming kiss that rocks me down to my toes. If his arm weren't around my waist, my knees would be buckling right now.

"We're together," he says, all the questions gone from his eyes. Leaving me at the door still breathing hard, he strides into the bedroom, and his duffel hits the floor. The reassuring thud of his boots as he returns to my side calms my racing heart. "I'll come back, Isabel. Ain't nothing gonna keep me away."

Connor

What the hell are you thinking? Staying another night in the same bed with Isabel?

This is a mistake. One I can't take back even if I wanted to. But that doesn't stop me from kicking myself the entire way to my truck. Isabel deserves better than me. So does the kid.

She only introduced us because she needed someone in her corner. Because she was alone. From the conversations we've had, Isabel's close friendships are mostly long distance. Her college roommate, Celia. A former coworker, Nancy, who moved to Los Angeles. And Leah, and there was no fucking way she could have called *her*. The woman slapped her in the face. Even if she did have a good reason—or thought she did—I can't help being a little angry.

Isabel needs someone who wasn't pieced back together with rods and pins and prayers. A man who doesn't have nightmares from the beating—and all the other shit he's seen after twenty years with the Bureau.

So why can't I walk away?

Because you're falling for her.

The truth hits me hard enough, I'm surprised my sunglasses stay on. If I'm not careful, I'll make it all the way to Love City before Isabel gets to sleep in her own bed again.

It takes me half an hour of winding through the busy streets of east Austin to reach the old, abandoned mall Veronica and Mitzi were held in, and when I roll to a stop, AJ's leaning against his F-150, arms crossed, and his Stetson hiding his eyes.

"About damn time," he says, pushing off the side of his vehicle. "Been waitin' here for almost an hour."

"That's on you. I told you I wasn't sure when I'd get out of there." It doesn't matter that I've only spent a handful of hours with AJ Stone. I can read him, and something heavy's weighing him down. Something other than this case and the loss of his wife. "Want to tell me what has your spurs on backwards?"

With a muttered curse, he shakes his head. "I shouldn't."

"If you always followed the rules, you wouldn't have dragged my dying ass out of Flash Flood Alley." When I stand in front of him, the strain is even more evident. "Did you sleep at all last night?"

"Got a solid five hours before Leah Nelson's protective detail had to take her to the hospital and place her under a seventy-two hour psych hold."

"Fuck. Why?" As soon as the question leaves my mouth, I kick myself.

Because her daughter's missing. Because Veronica got away. Because seeing Isabel yesterday didn't help her a damn bit.

"Don't answer that. I can figure it out. Her detail still in place?" Another question I shouldn't have asked from the look AJ gives me. "I'll tell Isabel. She'll want to know. Any updates on Reggie Boswell, *Officer* Milton, or Mitzi?"

Following him to the exterior door that's secured with a crime scene sticker, I wait for him to break the seal. "Milton hasn't been to work since Tuesday. Executed a search of his apartment, but it was clean. And very empty. He's in the wind. Boswell's been in and out of prison for half his life. Drug trafficking, assault, pimping, possession of stolen property…"

"*Pimping?* Fuck. If he sells Mitzi—"

"He won't." AJ folds up his pocket knife with a snort. "The dumbfuck got run out of the business by the big dogs. Word from one of our CIs is that if he ever tries to pimp a girl again, he'll end up missing a vital part of his anatomy."

Thank God. Isabel and Veronica don't need that worry on top of everything else.

The mall is utterly silent, the emergency lights chasing the darkness into the far corners of the main concourse. AJ unbuttons his jacket to rest his hand on his pistol and motions for me to stay behind him.

Great. Like I needed the reminder I'm no better than a civilian.

I tug at the collar of my flannel shirt. One good thing about being on leave? No dress code. "Don't suppose your CI has any idea where Boswell is hiding?"

AJ stops, turns very slowly on his heel, and removes his hat. Fuck. If that's not a sure sign he's madder than a hornet, I don't know what is. "Do you think I'd be *here* right now if we knew where Boswell was? The girl would be back with her mother, Isabel and Veronica would be home, and I wouldn't be lying to my chief every four hours 'bout where half my unit got off to."

Holding up my hands, I take a step back. "You're right. I'm an asshole with trust issues. I'm not used to bein' on the sidelines, and I'm not handlin' it well. You want to take a swing at me, go ahead."

"I ain't *that* much of a dick," he mutters. "Even if you deserve it. But give me a little credit. If there's a major development, I'm gonna call you."

My phone buzzes in my back pocket, and once AJ dons his hat, I check the screen. "It's Zephyr. She ID'd the guy who tried to kill Veronica in the hospital. His name's Danny Wilbur. Milton arrested him for possession a few years back, but he got off on a technicality. Sendin' you all the info she found on him."

With a few taps, I transfer the file, and AJ forwards it to one of his guys. "If we're lucky, he'll be in custody within the hour."

"Lucky? Have you ever drawn the best bull?"

AJ chuckles. "Not since I met my wife. But you're gettin' cozy with Isabel. That seems pretty damn lucky to me."

Lights flicker as we move through the dilapidated building. The girls were held in an old Top Shot sporting goods store, and when we get close, we both draw our weapons. Luck can change on a dime.

The space is silent save for the buzz of the fluorescents, and once we've cleared the front and back rooms, AJ points to a messy corner covered in print dust. "Mitzi and Veronica were both fingerprinted as part of some *Stranger Danger* campaign when they were in middle school. That covers more than half of what we found. The others weren't in the system."

"Whose system? You able to search outside your own database?"

"Austin PD gives us access. But that's it." He pulls off his hat and runs a hand through his dark brown hair. "If you can pull any strings with the Bureau—"

"I was thinking of something a little less...official."

AJ narrows his eyes at me. "You do that, you're on your own. Don't tell me about it, don't leave any trace of it on anything you send me, and for the love of God, don't say a word about it in front of any of my unit. You shouldn't even be *here* right now, but I can explain that away if I have to. Anythin' more? I'll be up shit creek without a paddle."

Nodding at the half-dozen sets of clear prints around the space, I don't say a word, and AJ huffs out a breath. "Gotta check somethin' in the back room."

As soon as he's out of sight, I snap as many pictures as I can before his heavy steps warn me to put my phone away. I'm about to stand up when I see a broken piece of plastic sticking out from under a dented set of shelves. No text or markings, but along one jagged edge of the beige triangle, a metallic sliver glints in the light.

Tucking it into my pocket, I clear my throat. "Ain't nothin' useful here. Any issue with me checkin' out the scene of the car accident?"

AJ frowns, staring at me like he knows I'm guilty of something, but he can't figure out what. After a beat, he shakes his head. "Nope. Knock yourself out. As soon as we find Officer Milton—still can't believe the damn fool used his real name at the hospital—or Danny Wilbur, I'll call you. Until then, stay out of trouble."

He makes a big show of locking and re-sealing the door with a fresh sticker once we're outside. Rolling down the window of his truck, he peers down at me. "You be careful, Connor. The Bureau can't protect you anymore."

He's right, even if I don't want to admit it. Getting the prints was worth the shit he gave me, but I can't win for losing. Just one more reminder that I'm a washed-up has been with no official authority to help anyone.

A TEN-MINUTE WALK from the mall, I understand why the assholes chasing Veronica couldn't get to her once she'd been hit by the car. The highway gets a shitton of traffic—even in the middle of the day. It's a risk—thinking no one's going to care that a man with an obvious limp is traipsing through the overgrown blue bonnets planted in the median—but dammit. She had her phone with her when she ran.

It's probably in pieces all over the highway by now. Tiny fragments of metal and glass scattered to the wind. But as far as I know, AJ and his team didn't search the area. A few pieces of gauze caught in the greenery lead me to where the EMTs worked on the kid before transporting her to the hospital. If the phone's anywhere, it's further down the road.

I cover a full half mile before I give up and turn around. Nothing. Until the sun glints off something on the other side of the road. It's only a few inches from the white line, and when traffic clears enough for me to cross, I can't contain my triumphant "hot damn."

The phone's still in its sparkly purple case, and while the screen's mostly gone—I can see the battery's logo through the missing glass—maybe Zephyr will be able to work a miracle.

CHAPTER FIFTEEN

Connor

Since I can't talk openly with Zephyr in front of Billings and McGrath, and I still have three hours before the best BBQ joint in Austin opens for dinner, I head back to my apartment.

Once I'm on the couch with an ice pack over my knee, I prop my tablet next to me and call Zephyr.

"About time," she says, splitting the screen before I can even say hello. "Meet Officer Walter Milton. Thirty-three years old, graduated middle of his class at the police academy, and has been written up for racial profiling, abuse of power, and reckless discharge of a firearm."

"Well, he's on a first name basis with the bottom of the deck."

Zephyr leans closer to the camera. "I know those words are all English, but hell if I can figure out what they mean."

With a chuckle, I shift the ice pack slightly. "You grow up in Texas, you pick up some rather...unique phrases. Just means he's a piece of shit."

"Now that one I understand." She tucks a lock of teal hair

behind her ear and rests her elbows on her knees. "He transferred to the Austin PD from Dallas six months ago. And Connor? You're going to want to prepare yourself for this next bit."

Prepare myself?

My palms go clammy in a heartbeat as photos of the two men I never wanted to see again appear next to Zephyr's face. The cops Alec convinced to go after me.

"They're dead," I manage through a jaw clenched so tight, my molars grind together. "Firefight with a couple of pissed off Rangers."

"I know. But they were Walter Milton's two best friends at the police academy. Along with this guy." A new photo fills the space, and thank fuck I don't have to look at those two assholes any longer. "Detective Thomas Archer. He's assigned to narcotics in San Marcos. And he hasn't been to work in three days."

"As in..."

"Not since Tuesday."

Neither of us utter a word for several long moments until I drop my head onto the back of the couch. "I'll show Veronica his photo when I go back to the safehouse. If he's the other guy from the mall—the one who grabbed Mitzi—we're gonna need to tell AJ. Don't suppose you can make it so all the intel you just shared with me falls into his lap in a *legal* manner?"

Zephyr rolls her eyes. "There isn't much I can't do, Connor. At least not when I pull in Wren or Ripper out in Seattle. I'm good. They're better."

The west coast K&R firm—Hidden Agenda—has not one, but two master hackers working for them, along with my brother's guy and several other former military heroes-turned-mercenaries.

"Are you good enough to fix a broken cell phone?" Holding up Veronica's mobile, I show Zephyr the screen.

"Does it power on?" she asks.

Dumbass. Why didn't I think of that? "The buttons are mostly...gone. Hang on. Let me get my charger."

I limp into my bedroom and sink down onto my bed to unplug my phone cable. The weight of seeing the two men who almost killed me hits—hard. After the first couple of strikes from the bat, everything's blurry, but their faces are burned into my memories. Digging my fingers into my thigh, I relish the pain. I need it to focus.

Zephyr's waiting. Get out of your own head.

Once I return to the living room, I plug in the phone and hold my breath. The device buzzes once, but no lights, no sounds.

"Well?" Zephyr asks.

"It vibrated. But most of the screen's gone. How the hell am I supposed to know if it works?" Tension gathers around my forehead like a vise. Dammit. I need my meds before the migraine that's been threatening for two days takes me down.

Zephyr stares at me like I don't have enough sense to spit downwind. "You call it?"

I'm an idiot. "I'll call Isabel's detail. They can get the number. Not sure what good that's gonna do us, though."

"Just send me the phone," Zephyr says. "I'll text you the account number and a local affiliate for our courier. Drop the phone off and tell them to overnight it to me with morning delivery."

"You expect me to leave this with a random courier? Hell, no. This could be the only evidence we have against those assholes."

She rolls her eyes. "Give me a little credit. The courier is licensed and bonded. More importantly, Hidden Agenda bought the company last year. They vet every employee."

Adjusting the ice pack to cover the back of my neck this time, something pokes me in the hip. The shard of plastic.

"Fine. Send me the info and I'll get you the phone. That's not all I have, though. I'm emailing you photos of the fingerprints from the mall where Veronica and Mitzi were held. AJ can't match them to anyone, but he doesn't have access to any federal databases. I reckon that won't be a problem for you?"

"If it is, Ripper can help." Zephyr scribbles something on a notepad, then laces her fingers together and stretches her hands above her head. "Damn. I need to start setting timers so I get up more than once every six hours. You got anything else for me?"

If I had any other way to find out what the fuck this thing is, I'd use it. Give the poor woman a break. "Need another set of eyes on somethin'."

"Show me." She yawns, and I finally notice the bags under her eyes.

"Zephyr, have you slept?" As desperate as I am for help, I can't let her run herself into the ground. Not when we still have so many unanswered questions.

"Don't worry about me. I'm used to this. Before I came to Boston, my sleep schedule was majorly fucked. What's the mystery item behind door number three?"

"This." I hold the beige plastic piece up to the camera and turn it so Zephyr can see all sides. "No markings, but is this part of a computer chip?"

"Webcams are shit for resolution. Snap a pic and text it to me?" she asks. As soon as she gets the photo, Zephyr shakes her head. "Not from a computer. That's an old school RFID sensor."

"Like in credit cards?"

She nods. "And in hotel room keys, building access cards, and a whole lot of other things. I don't suppose you're on good terms with any local geeks, are you? Like at the Bureau?"

"Not good enough."

"Then send me the card along with the phone. Make *sure* the courier knows to put both of them in Faraday bags before shipping. I might be able to pull something off the sensor." She starts typing, and a few seconds later, my phone vibrates with the courier's address and a sixteen-digit account number. "Make sure you get these out by seven or they won't get here until tomorrow afternoon. I'll run the prints across every database I can find, and when I get something, you'll be the first to know."

She ends the video call, and I close my eyes, letting the ice pack soothe my aching head. I may be less than useless these days, but at least I have capable friends.

Isabel

Doing nothing? It makes me want to crawl out of my skin. Or worse. Go running. Veronica hasn't left the couch all day other than to use the bathroom, and I've stayed by her side the whole time. Binge-watching an entire season of *Baking Wars*? Not how I usually spend my time.

I wish I could talk to Leah. Or check in with work. Or do *anything* but sit here and pray a group of Texas Rangers I don't know can find Mitzi, arrest the men who hurt her and my baby girl, and make us safe again.

A little after 6:00 p.m., when I'm walking what feels like my thousandth circuit around the apartment, there's a knock at the door, and both Billings and McGrath jump to their feet.

"It's me. Open up," Connor says, and I'm so happy to hear his voice, I sprint the half a dozen steps from the living room to the alcove just inside the door.

The fluttering in my belly intensifies when I see him. Same flannel shirt. Same Wranglers. Same boots. But he locks eyes with me, and the heat in his gaze? It hits me hard enough to take my breath away.

"You all right, darlin'?" He drops the large paper bag with *Emmit's BBQ* emblazoned on the side and wraps his arm around my waist.

"Better now." Our kiss lasts long enough Billings clears his throat from behind Connor, and my cheeks flush hot. "God, that was incredibly cheesy, wasn't it?"

He chuckles, reaching for the bag and guiding me to the kitchen. "Don't be knockin' cheese. It's worthy of its own food group. And there's a double order of grits in this bag."

"*Emmit's BBQ?*" Veronica's gets up with a little groan and shoves her crutch under her arm. "They make you order a week in advance. Or wait in line for hours." She limps into the kitchen, eyes as wide as saucers. "Mom...you *have* to keep Connor around. He brings the best food!"

Can I disappear through a hole in the floor now? Or banish my daughter to her room for the next thousand years?

While I want to die of embarrassment, Connor laughs, pulling container after container from the bag and lining them up on the counter. "The owner's a friend. But even that wouldn't have been enough on a Saturday night. Go easy on me with tomorrow's dinner order, lil' bit. Somethin' simple."

"I don't even care," she says, her eyes sparkling when she gets a peek at the five-pound container of brisket. "This is worth peanut butter and jelly sandwiches for a whole *week*."

"I'm going to remember you said that." I smooth a hand over her thick locks. She only cried twice today, but between these moments of pure, teenage joy, she's falling apart with worry and guilt, and it kills me that I can't "kiss it and make it better" like I used to.

At least she lets me fix her a plate. Her good mood lasts until she tries to pick up the roll stuffed with brisket and sauce. Half the contents land on the plate with a *splat*, and tears gather in her eyes.

I'm about to tell her it's okay when Connor stops with his

own roll halfway to his mouth. Without missing a beat, he dumps it onto his plate, grabs his fork, and winks at Veronica. "This is the only way to mop up all the sauce."

I follow suit, and even Billings and McGrath—who are eating at the counter so they can keep an eye on the front door—switch to forks.

She can't argue with all of us, so she gives in, and once again, I'm in awe of this man who showed up when I needed him—without question—and still hasn't run away from the mess our lives have become.

AFTER DINNER, Connor sets a small backpack on the bed in what I guess is "our" room and shuts the door. "Burner phone," he says, passing me something that looks like it belongs in a museum. "I got four of them. No GPS, and while they're not untraceable, the numbers aren't linked to you in any way. You can call your office and Veronica's school with the same phone, then turn it off and remove the battery—here."

"Is that really necessary?"

"Yes." The sharp word shocks me, and he must realize it, because he cups my cheek and urges me to meet his gaze. "Isabel, I won't take any chances with your safety." Scooting closer, he touches his forehead to mine and lowers his voice. "I found Veronica's cell phone today."

"What?" At my exclamation, he flinches, his hand moving to the back of my neck to hold me in place.

"Billings and McGrath can't know about this. It was half destroyed, but there might be enough left for Zephyr to access the videos Veronica took."

Connor shifts, stretching his legs out on the bed and tugging me against him. I've never felt as safe as I do in his arms, even when he tells me about Leah.

"I wish I could see her. Or do something. *Anything* besides sit here all day watching reality TV and drinking too much coffee."

His laugh rumbles through me, and when his hands skim down my arms to rest on my hips, I glance at the door. Veronica's right on the other side watching TV. "If Zephyr's as good as Austin says she is, she'll have everythin' off her phone by noon tomorrow. Then, it's only a matter of time before that asshole drug dealer shows up on a security camera."

"How does that help?"

"Zephyr can match a face in under ten minutes. He won't be able to hide for long."

Turning, I frown when I catch sight of the lines of pain bracketing his lips. "What's wrong? You look like you've been chewed up, spit out, and stepped on."

"Fighting a migraine. Happens when I don't sleep. That...or the halos." He closes his eyes with a heavy sigh. "I took somethin' before I left home. Should be fine in the morning."

The knock at the door surprises us both, and I jerk out of his arms when Veronica calls, "Mom? Can you help me get ready for bed?"

"Coming, baby girl." The few steps to the door feel like a mile. I don't want to leave his side, but my daughter needs me, and she has to come first—even before me. I pause with my hand on the knob and glance back at Connor. His eyes are still closed, and he looks relaxed for the first time since he showed up at the hospital. I'm not waiting until "this is all over" to tell him how I feel. Or show him. I can't. Life is too short.

CHAPTER SIXTEEN

Connor

HARDISON AND ELMORE show up as Isabel slips out of Veronica's room. "She *hates* that cast with a passion she usually reserves for pop quizzes and her alarm clock."

"Just wait until it starts to itch." Scratching at my forearm, the memories so close to the surface I can taste them, I swallow hard when I find the thick scars from multiple surgeries. "I'll bring her a pair of extra-long chopsticks tomorrow."

Isabel narrows her eyes at me. "She's not supposed to—"

Chuckling, I reach out to link our fingers. "Of course, she isn't. But do you think that's going to stop her? Might as well make it as easy and safe as possible."

Elmore, whose first name I think might be Parker, starts a pot of coffee and leans against the counter, her arms crossed. "He's right. I broke my leg a couple of years ago, and within a week, I was so desperate, I lost a ruler inside my cast. Had to snag it with a pair of knitting needles. The looks I got from the ladies at the craft store when I braced my crutches on the counter to pay for a pair of extra-long, skinny needles?" She snorts and rolls her eyes. "If I hadn't been about to crawl out of my own skin, I would have died on the spot."

"Y'all are *not* making me feel better."

"Consider it a rite of passage," I say, tugging her against me. "At least the knee brace will be off in a couple of weeks. I'd be surprised if she needed the crutch more than another day or two."

Some of the tension leaves Isabel's body and she slides her fingers through one of my belt loops. It's a surprisingly intimate gesture—like we've been together for years instead of days—and suddenly, I need to get her alone. Even if we can't *do* anything with Veronica in the next room, I still need her close. Preferably on top of me. In my arms. Kissing me.

"Knock if you need anything," I say with a nod to Elmore.

"See you in the morning," she replies, the light in her eyes telling me she knows *exactly* why I don't want anyone barging in. I don't care. I need Isabel like I need oxygen, and tonight, I intend to tell her.

IN OUR ROOM, she sinks down onto the bed and rubs her hands up and down her thighs. "I'm so tired, but I have all this nervous energy."

"I might be able to help with that," I say, removing my boots, belt, and gun. "Stretch out on your stomach. I seem to remember you liked the last massage I gave you."

"Oh, God." She practically purrs when my hands stroke up from her waist all the way to her shoulders. Digging my fingers into the tight knots, I lean down and press a kiss to her neck and she shivers. "Do that again."

"What? This?" Another kiss, this one closer to her ear. "Tasting you? It's somethin' I could get used to."

A shudder runs through her entire body as her muscles

loosen under my touch. Despite the tightness of my Wranglers, I straddle her, stifling my groan when my dick strains against my zipper. Working my hands lower, bold, slow strokes all the way down to her ass, I say a silent prayer she doesn't ask me to stop.

With every knot I find, she moans, and I lean closer to score my teeth over the shell of her ear. "Might want to grab a pillow, darlin'. Wouldn't want to wake Veronica."

Isabel jerks, a little gasp escaping her lips before she takes one of the fluffy pillows and buries her face in it. The moans are quieter now, but the added buffer seems to free her from the tight control she has on her emotions, and her body comes alive.

As I work my fingers along her hips, she writhes, swiveling her lower body until I can't take it anymore. Kneeling next to her, I roll her over, then cage her with my arms so my lips are only a few inches from hers. "I want you, darlin'."

"So, take me." The challenge in her gaze should be enough, and if we were in any other situation, I'd be stripping off her sweater and worshipping her breasts by now, but Isabel deserves so much more than a hurried fuck with the threat of interruption hanging over our heads.

She trails her hand down my chest, all the way to the button on my jeans. Flicking it open, a wicked grin curving her lips, she moves to the zipper.

"Do I have to beg? Because I will."

Fuuuuck. How am I supposed to resist her when her voice takes on that deep, sultry tone and she strokes delicate fingers over the hard bulge straining against my boxers?

"Are you sure?" I have to force the words out with her touching me like that. It's been too long since a woman *wanted* me. Since I let *myself* want. "We're not alone here."

"Veronica won't come in. She was out the second she got into bed. I need this, Connor. I need you."

No one ever accused me of being dumb as a post—at least not where women are concerned—so I slide off the bed and quietly flick the lock on the door.

When I turn around, I lose my words entirely. Isabel's standing in only her bra and panties, and though they're plain —just black silk from what I can tell—they frame her body in a way that pushes *all* my buttons.

Including the one that makes these Wranglers so tight, I'm afraid if I don't get them off soon, I'll do permanent damage. But before I can tell her that, she drops her gaze to the floor. "I'm scared, Connor."

I reach her in two strides, but she shies away from me and holds up her hand.

"I'm forty-six years old. My boobs are starting to sag, I'm a good thirty pounds heavier than I was the last time I was naked in front of anyone other than my doctor, and now that we're actually here, I keep asking myself if I even remember *how* to be intimate with a man."

"Now hold up a minute." I take her hands in mine, rubbing my thumbs in gentle circles over the insides of her wrists. "You are hotter than blue blazes, Isabel Lopez, and if anyone has *ever* made you feel otherwise, I'm gonna have words with them. Ain't nothin' here even a fraction short of perfection."

Isabel's cheeks darken, and she glances back at the light. "We can—"

"Nope." Planting a swift, hard kiss to her lips, I release her. "Been a long time since I knocked boots with anyone, darlin'. Had the chance, sure. But this—sex—means somethin' to me. Always has. My mama drilled that into me when I was growing up, and I sure as shit ain't gonna change my ways now."

Her eyes glisten, and I can't tell if she's about to cry or if she's as turned on as I am. Hoping for the latter, I start undoing the buttons on my shirt and offer her an encouraging smile.

"Also, pretty sure this is like ridin' a bike. But if ain't, we'll figure it out together. Been a while for me too."

"Ten years?" Now, there's a challenge swirling with the desire in her gaze. Her hands skim over my pecs and ease the flannel down my arms before she presses a kiss to my left shoulder, turning me towards the light. "This is beautiful."

The phoenix inked all the way down my left arm is new—part of my recovery from the injuries that almost took my life—and having her trail kisses along the majestic bird's wings is both a comfort and the sexiest damn thing I've ever seen.

"Had to do something to prove I lived through the last four months." My voice is rough, the Wranglers strangling my dick every time I shift—or breathe.

"If I don't get these jeans off soon, I'm gonna be in a world of hurt, darlin'." I hook my thumbs in my belt loops, but my mouth falls open when Isabel drops to her knees and tugs the denim down my legs. She's eye level with the very obvious tent in my boxers, and shit. I don't want her on her knees. She deserves to be worshipped.

"On the bed, darlin'. We're not *there* yet."

"This is for both of us, remember?" she asks. "You don't know what I like."

Inclining my head, I offer her my hand and help her up. "So tell me. While I taste you."

"Connor!" she yelps when I scoop her up in my arms and set her in the center of the bed. "Please tell me that wasn't as loud as I think it was..."

"It *probably* didn't carry into the next room," I say with a grin. At Isabel's horrified expression, I trail my knuckle along her cheek. "We can stop. No reason to hurry. I ain't goin' nowhere."

"I don't want to stop." Trailing her fingers over my chest, she traces the scar just under my ribs. "If this whole terrible situation has taught me anything, it's that life is too short to wait for the perfect time for *anything*. If we're ever safe again—" A low growl vibrates in my chest, and she corrects herself. "When we're safe, I'm going to cook you dinner. We're opening the good bottle of wine. And then I'll light the expensive candles on the white silk tablecloth that's been in the cabinet since I bought it, and if either one of us spills the blackberry cobbler, so be it."

"Blackberry cobbler, huh?" I slide one of her bra straps off her shoulder so I can kiss a line from her collarbone to her ear. "Sounds mighty fine, darlin'. Better than perfect. Just like you."

Straddling her, I let her feel how much I want her—how much I need her.

Her nipples pebble under the black silk and I dip my head to fasten my lips around one tight nub. Isabel arches her back, and the position allows me to slip a hand under her and flick open the bra catch. "So about what you like," I murmur when there's nothing between us but her panties.

"That's....oh yes." Tangling her fingers in my hair, she twists the short strands until the first pinpricks of pain dance along the back of my head. "Don't make the other one jealous."

I laugh and toss the bra to the floor. "Wouldn't dream of it." My tongue traces a lazy circle around the dusky skin, and goosebumps race down her neck all the way to her mound. "Harder? Softer?"

"Harder. Definitely harder." Her voice spurs me on, driving me to score my teeth over the rosy bud. Isabel claps her hand over her mouth and moans. Fuuuuck. If that isn't the sexiest sound I've ever heard...

I explore her body, kissing a trail down to the top of her panties. "You're perfect, darlin'. And God, you smell amazing."

Once she's bared to me, dark curls glistening with the sweetest scent to grace this earth, I peer up at her. "Might want to grab that pillow again before I taste you."

She does, hiding her half-lidded eyes, parted lips, and unfocused gaze. Soon, we're gonna do this without anyone else around, but for now, it's enough that we're here. That we're together.

Her body trembles as I spread her thighs with my hands and drag my tongue through her slick folds. I hope to all that's holy I haven't forgotten what a woman likes, and when I find her clit, her muffled cry reassures me in ways I didn't know I needed.

Pure, raw desire shoots down to my dick, and it's been so long, I don't know if I'll last once I'm inside of her. "Gonna make you come now." The vibration of my lips against her sweet spot has her heels digging into the mattress, and she hugs the pillow tighter.

Two fingers plunge inside her, twisting to find her G-spot as I increase the pressure with my tongue. Every muscle in her body coils and tightens, like she's an exquisite instrument tuned just for me.

Her words are a mystery, but the way she flies when she lets go? It's nothing short of breathtaking.

Isabel

I'd forgotten what it was like to be loved. To have someone put my desires above theirs. To care about my physical needs as well as my emotional ones. Tremors wrack my body as I come down from the high of my release, and I push the pillow aside so I can meet Connor's gaze.

He's moved. No longer between my legs, he cradles me like I'm the most precious flower. He's fast becoming my home. My rock. My anchor in this violent storm threatening to drown me.

My chest heaves, but though my heart still hammers

against my ribs like I just finished an all-out sprint, my muscles are so languid, I might as well be boneless.

"Back with me, darlin'?" he asks, his lips fluttering against the shell of my ear. "Wouldn't want to lose you."

"You can't lose me. I'm yours." I don't know where the words come from. They're too much. Too soon. But that makes them no less true.

His eyes widen, and just when I'm about to fumble my way through an apology, the corners of his mouth twitch into a smile. "I like the sound of that."

His hard length presses to my hip, and I wriggle onto my side until we're facing one another. "You don't think we're done, do you?" Stroking my hand over the bulge in his boxers, I giggle —and when did I last giggle?—at the way his eyes roll back in his head. "Off with these. I want to see you."

"Yes, ma'am." His voice is rough, and he almost topples over when he rolls off the bed to standing. But the boxers land on the floor next to my bra and panties, and his arousal juts proudly from trimmed, dark hair sprinkled with gray. I lick my lips, and his shoulders straighten.

"Did you think I'd be disappointed?" I ask, sitting up and guiding him between my legs. "Because you're a tall drink of water on a hot day, Connor Davis, and I'm going to drink you down."

His knees falter, but I don't hesitate to wrap my lips around him. The velvety heat against my tongue, the tang of salt, and his muttered curses and grunts as I hollow out my cheeks are life itself as I try to give him a fraction of the pleasure he gave me.

My nipples brush along his thighs, one arm tight around his hip. I don't know where this brazen, daring version of me came from. All I know is I don't want to ever forget how amazing it feels to have this strong, caring, capable man turn to putty in my hands.

"Isabel..." he manages, and I'm so turned on, so wet, I can't wait to feel him inside me. It's slow torture to release him—for both of us—and when I tip my head up to meet his gaze, the depth of emotion in his eyes takes my breath away. "Lie back."

It's not a request. This is an order. A very firm—yet still tender—order.

Moving to the center of the bed, I watch the way his corded muscles flex as he digs in his duffel bag and comes away with a condom clutched in his fingers.

"You were a Boy Scout, weren't you?"

After he sheaths himself, Connor chuckles and climbs on the bed to straddle me. "Maybe. Or just hopeful."

"Well, now you're mine." Grabbing him by the hips, I position him at my entrance. "I want you, Connor. All of you. And I don't want to wait another second."

That's all he needs. With a low growl, his crown slips inside me, and God, I'm so tight, it feels like he's about to split me in two. But the burn as my inner walls stretch around him is the most delicious kind of pain, and I dig my fingers into the hard muscles of his ass and pull him closer.

He buries himself deep with a single, hard thrust, and I wrap my legs around him—as much for leverage as to let him know I can take whatever he can give. I'm his as much as he's mine, and in this moment, there's nothing but the two of us together.

Connor braces one hand on the headboard and with the other, reaches between us to find my clit. The pressure as he rubs circles around the magic bundle of nerves is such sweet torture, I hope he never stops.

"I can't get enough of you, darlin'," he whispers, leaning down to claim my lips. He's so close, his cock surging into me with every hard thrust, and when he bites down on my lower lip, I let myself go, taking Connor with me.

CHAPTER SEVENTEEN

Connor

Light filters in through a crack in the drapes. Isabel sighs, curled against me with her arms wrapped around a pillow.

It had been so long for both of us, we were far from sated by our first round. After an hour cuddling and sharing bits of our past—how Quinton and I had once been close, how she'd coped the first couple of years alone with a grieving pre-teen, my first assignment with the FBI—I'd been unable to keep my hands off her, and I'm mighty glad I bought a whole box of condoms yesterday.

As soon as I try to ease out of bed, she stirs, stretching in such a way her breasts—covered by her purple tank top—tent the sheet. Fuck. If I don't put some distance between us, I'm gonna take her again, and I can hear Veronica moving around in the main room. The sound of a crutch clicking with each step is something I'll never forget. But I pause to brush my lips to Isabel's cheek. "Morning, darlin'. Stay here and I'll bring you coffee."

"You're my hero," she murmurs, her voice still thick with

sleep—and all the muffled screams I wrung from her body last night. "But I should check on V."

"She's up. Probably trying to convince Elmore to teach her all those swear words in ASL. I'll see if she needs anythin'."

Isabel frowns as she scoots up to rest her back against the headboard and mutters, "She's almost an adult. I need to remember that."

"She's also your kid. You're allowed to worry about her no matter how old she is. Hell, I still worry about Quinton every damn day and he's a grown-ass man with a whole group of mercenaries as his second family. Shit. I need to call him today, too." After I tug on a t-shirt and my Wranglers, I run a hand through my hair, hoping I don't look like I ravaged Isabel for hours last night.

With a sigh, Isabel snags her bra from the floor. "She's my whole world, Connor. Almost everything good in my life is tied to her."

Leaning over, I cup her cheek and skate my thumb over the fading bruise. "I know. And I'll do everythin' I can to keep her safe. Including getting you coffee so you don't tear Elmore a new one."

Isabel laughs, and it's a sound I hope I hear every damn day for the rest of my life. The realization slams into me like a freight train, and I have to get out of this room before I admit I'm falling hard and fast. Or before she takes off her shirt to put on that bra.

Veronica leans against the kitchen counter, shoveling cereal into her mouth at a truly impressive pace. When I grab two coffee mugs from the cabinet, she sets her spoon down and stares at me. "So...you and my mom..."

"Fuck me," I mutter under my breath as I pour the coffee. It's a good thing Isabel stayed in the bedroom. Taking a sip gives me an extra few seconds to form a reply that won't get me murdered by either Veronica *or* her mother. "I like her. A lot. And we're...together. That what you wanted to know?"

"Nope."

"I reckon I should ask your mom what *she* thinks before I shoot my mouth off." The angry rumble coming from my stomach reminds me that sex—especially the mind-blowing, all-consuming, hot as fuck sex we had last night—is a hell of a workout. Rummaging in the cabinet, I come away with a package of powdered donuts to split with Isabel. Before I take two steps, Veronica stands up a little straighter.

"There are donuts?"

The look on her face? Like it's Christmas morning and she just found out Santa is real. "Knock yourself out, lil' bit. We've got more."

She tears the package open with her teeth, and I should have realized it would be hard for her one handed. But before I can apologize, she grins at me, powdered sugar coating her lips. "You're cool. And you make my mom happy."

"Is 'cool' still good?" I arch a brow at the kid, and she laughs.

"It's good. Just don't break her heart, okay?"

With a nod, I gather the two mugs in one hand and tuck the donuts in the crook of my arm. "I'd have to kick my own ass if I did. No one's gonna hurt either of you if I can help it."

Isabel

By the time I help my daughter shower and dress, then make myself presentable, it's almost eleven.

"Mom, can you call the school now?" Veronica asks, her tone way too whiny for a girl who, less than an hour ago, told me she could brush her own hair, then changed her mind after five strokes.

"If you fix your attitude, I can."

"Sorry." Staring down at her leg encased in that God-awful brace, she picks at the edge of her cast with her good hand. "I'd really appreciate it if you called the school. And maybe...Mitzi's mom?"

Every part of me wants to take Veronica in my arms and find a way to make it all better. But I can't. Not anymore, and definitely not with this. "Mitzi's mom is having a hard time, baby girl. I don't think she wants to hear from me right now. But when Connor talks to AJ later on, he'll ask about her. Let me grab one of the burner phones and I'll call Mrs. Chandler at the Academy."

He's fresh out of the shower when I slip into the bedroom we share and shut the door behind me. Bare-ass naked, he lunges for the towel draped over the headboard, but I get there first.

"You *do* remember I saw all of you last night?" Holding the bath sheet just out of reach, I take a moment to appreciate all six-foot-three inches of toned man in front of me.

His cheeks turn the most interesting shade of red, but in the next moment, a pure, almost primal need darkens his eyes, and he stalks toward me. "Might recall somethin' of the sort."

I retreat until my back is against the door and Connor cages me with his arms. Heat rolls off him, and my nipples tighten under my soft red sweater. "I could refresh your memory." Trailing my hand down his chest, over his *very* chiseled eight pack, and down to his cock, I relish the way he groans softly, then slants his mouth over mine.

With bold strokes of his tongue, he claims me—there's no other word for it—and if I could, I'd grab him by his impressive length and steer him right to the bed.

By the time Connor releases me, I'm breathless, and my

core aches in a way I'm not sure I've ever felt before. "That was...wow."

Chuckling, he pinches one of my nipples until I have to stifle my squeal. "Wow?"

"Don't mock me, stud. Or there will be no *knockin' boots* tonight."

He backs away, hands in the air. "Zipping it. Understood." With a wink, he adds, "Kinda like it when you call me 'stud.'"

"Give me one of those burner phones and I'll do it again. Stud." I shouldn't joke around when my daughter's life is in danger, but I need this. A shred of normalcy in this very *abnormal* situation.

Connor tugs on a fresh pair of boxer shorts—green this time—and rummages through his duffel bag for a t-shirt. "One call per number per phone," he says. "I doubt these assholes have the resources or the brains to run a trace, but I'm not takin' any chances."

"I need to have the Academy make a list of Veronica's assignments, then call my boss and let him know why I haven't checked in for three days." Sinking down on the bed, I drop my head into my hands. "I love my job. And I'm good at it. But if I'd never started working for Second Chances, Mitzi and Veronica would be at the library right now. I'd be having coffee with Leah and talking about...nothing in particular."

The mattress dips, and Connor drapes his arm around my shoulders. "I'd do just about anythin' to change the past, darlin'. Be a better brother. A better son. A better man. But I can't."

"The past led us here," I say quietly. "And as much as I wish most of the past few days had never happened, there's one part of *here* I don't want to live without." Raising my head, I meet Connor's gaze. "Us."

THE ACADEMY PRINCIPAL—WHO bless her heart was actually *working* on a Saturday—promised to have Veronica's assignments put together by 5:00 p.m., and she's happily flopped on the couch binging the most absurd reality show on the planet —*Extreme Obstacle Course.* In the kitchen, I lean against the counter, staring out the tiny window at the top of the next building. An exhaust fan mesmerizes me until the call connects and my boss's executive assistant answers.

"Roger Haskel's office. How can I help you?"

"Maggie? It's Isabel Lopez. What are you doing in on the weekend? I thought I'd be talking to Roger's voicemail. Is he actually working today?"

"He's at lunch with one of our Platinum-level donors, but we've been trying to get in touch with you for two days. Luke's in the office as well. He can explain what they need. Can I transfer you?"

I roll my eyes. Luke is the *last* person I want to talk to, but the office hold music plays briefly. Dammit. She didn't even wait for me to answer.

"Isabel? Finally. Where the hell have you been?" Luke's voice grates, his holier-than-thou tone not what I need right now.

"My daughter was in a car accident. I'm sorry if that's been *inconvenient* for you, but she needed me. Still does."

"I went to your house yesterday. No one was home."

"Why, thank you for being so concerned with Veronica's well-being. Or mine, for that matter."

Connor pokes his head out of the bedroom, his phone pressed to his ear. "Hang on, AJ. Everythin' okay, darlin'?"

"Just need to remind one of my colleagues what *manners* are."

"Isabel," Luke says, again with the patronizing, calm, almost sing-song voice. "The New Dawn Foundation rejected our grant application!"

"What? On what grounds?" I went over that proposal for hours Monday and Tuesday and submitted it well before the deadline.

"I don't know. You handle all that stuff. But Roger's pissed, and if we don't fix it by tomorrow, they'll allocate the funds to someone else. You have to come in and fix this."

"I can't 'come in.' Veronica needs me here."

"Then I'll come to you. Bring your laptop and whatever else you need. This can't wait, Isabel. They practically assured Roger the grant would have already been ours had you followed the rules."

Oh, you little shit. I followed every single one of the rules.

I have half a mind to tell Luke he can go fuck himself, but what else am I going to do here all day besides work? Watch hour after hour of reality television? "I'll be in later this afternoon to get my laptop and my paper files. I can't stay, but once I have my stuff, I can fix the application from here. Tell Roger it'll be done by morning."

"What time will you get here?" he asks.

"I don't know. When I can. I have to find someone to stay with Veronica." That's a bald-faced lie. Veronica has two Texas Rangers with her at all times, but I'm not sharing that with Luke. "Before five. And if anyone tries to guilt me into staying, they can fix the damn application themselves."

Jabbing the screen, I hang up on him before pulling the battery from the back of the phone like Connor told me to.

He ambles into the kitchen, and the crease between his brows is a hell of a lot deeper than it was just a few minutes ago. "That didn't sound 'okay' to me, darlin'."

"I need to go to my office," I say quietly, so Veronica won't hear me. After I fill him in on the bits of the phone call he didn't hear, I curl my hands around his hips and meet his gaze. "Will you take me?"

He blows out a long, slow breath. "I don't like the idea of you leaving the apartment."

"Neither do I. Not really. Even though I'm going a little stir crazy just sitting here. But you'll protect me." His shoulders straighten—just slightly—and I press closer to him. "I feel safe with you."

CHAPTER EIGHTEEN

Connor

AN UNSEASONABLY WARM breeze ruffles Isabel's hair as I pull off I-35. With the windows rolled down and the radio blasting, the drive to the little diner where Brent's waiting felt like the most normal thing in the world. But now that we're almost there, Isabel's shoulders hike up to her ears, and she clutches her purse strap like it's a lifeline.

"What's wrong, darlin'?" Reaching across the center console, I cover her fingers with mine, and she forces out a breath.

"I didn't think it would be this hard to leave Veronica. She's so independent. Before...*everything*...I let her take the bus all the time. Or go to the library with Mitzi, out shopping..." Isabel's voice cracks, and she twists the leather strap tighter. "She has two highly trained Texas Rangers ten feet away from her. And all I can think about is how she can't call me if she needs me."

After I pull into a parking space at the edge of the diner's lot, I unlock my phone and pass it to her. "SHI is McGrath's number. SH2 is Elmore. You can call and check on Veronica any time you want."

The gratitude in her eyes makes my heart ache, but she hands the phone back to me and shakes her head. "I *know* she's okay. That she's safe. If I call her now, she'll accuse me of smothering her."

"If you change your mind—" Zephyr's name appears on the screen as the device starts to vibrate, and I accept the call. "Tell me you have somethin' from Veronica's phone," I say the second the video connects.

"Good morning to you too." She's wrapped in a blanket, still in the same position on the couch she was the last time we talked. And those bags under her eyes? They're darker than before.

"Sorry."

Isabel scoots closer. "Zephyr, don't take this the wrong way, but you look like I feel. Terrible. Are you okay?"

Surprise registers on Zephyr's face for a moment before she picks up a large mug and cups it in her hands. "I'm well enough. When this is all over, though, I might sleep for a week."

"I'll make sure of it," Ronan says from just off screen. "And we're turnin' the second bedroom into an office for you. One with a better chair and its own tea station."

Zephyr beams at him, and even on the tiny screen, her love for Ronan is unmistakable. "Austin's paying. He owes me after starting me off with a case like this."

Clearing my throat, I bring her attention back to the call. "Not to be an asshole, but my boss is waiting for us. You found somethin'?"

"I found the Holy Grail of treasures on that phone," she says. "It wasn't easy. I had to clone the thing and even then, it was so damaged, the files wouldn't open. But Ripper was able to help me repair them. Sending them to you now. Three videos and five still shots." The notification banner flashes at the top of the screen, and she takes a sip from her mug, then continues. "Veronica's one brave kid, Isabel. She was close enough you can *hear* Boswell hitting the woman—Jamie?—and their entire conversation is crystal clear. It's enough to put him away for... well...a long damn time. Milton too. And another one of her videos? Crystal clear view of Archer throwing Mitzi over his shoulder as she screamed."

"Hot damn. Don't suppose you have any idea how to get this to AJ...legally?" I ask. "Veronica can swear to the video's authenticity, but her phone didn't go through anythin' *close* to proper chain of custody."

Zephyr rolls her eyes. "I told you I could take care of that. In under an hour, one of his CIs will call in a tip and they'll find Veronica's phone between the mall and the highway."

"But you have it." Isabel's confusion mirrors my own. "How are they gonna—?"

"I have *a* phone. Who's to say the phone found *isn't* Veronica's? If the serial number matches what's on record with your carrier, AJ can use the videos with a clear conscience."

"And how is any phone gonna get where it needs to be?" My inner voice warns me to stop, to trust this woman who's proven herself a hundred times over in less than three days, but this is too important to leave anything to chance.

Ronan leans into the frame, his stare boring into me from two thousand miles away. "Same way you were dragged out of Flash Flood Alley ten minutes before you drowned. Jasper's already on his way."

"Take a breath," Zephyr says as she reaches up to cup Ronan's cheek. "Connor's just worried about Isabel and Veronica. Did *you* trust every word out of Dax's mouth when I was... missing?" Her voice trembles slightly, but she offers the man a smile, and he dips his head to kiss her lightly. "Go for a run or something. I've got this." The Irishman doesn't look happy, but he nods and disappears down the hall. "He's just pissy he woke up alone this morning."

"No, he's right. I owe you an apology." Draping my arm around Isabel's shoulders, I pull her as close as I can with the console between us. "You've done everythin' you promised and more. I'll never be able to repay you for any of this."

"Oh, you will. One day." The call drops before I get a chance to ask her about that strange piece of plastic or to clarify exactly how I'm paying her back, but Brent's waiting, and with the videos she sent me, I might be able to convince him to help us find Boswell and put an end to the asshole for good.

BRENT'S HALFWAY through his plate of chicken and waffles when we slide into the booth across from him. "'Bout damn time y'all showed up," he mutters.

"What I have is worth the wait." Entering the decryption code for the special comms app Zephyr insisted I use for all our exchanges, I bring up the first video she recovered.

"You think the police will believe *you?*" Boswell asks. In front of him, a slight woman with long brown hair swipes at her cheeks, her tears glistening in the lights from the sporting goods store. "Not likely."

"I'm clean! I've been clean for six months. Please—"

The crack of his fist to Jamie's jaw makes Isabel jerk, and I wrap my arm around her waist and tug her against me. On screen, Milton looms over the crumpled woman and jams a gun to her temple. "My duty log says otherwise, bitch. Five times I've caught you high as a fucking kite, and the next? You'll have enough smack on you for a felony conviction."

"I can't go back to that life," she sobs. "I'd rather die."

"That can be arranged." With a swift kick to her abdomen, Boswell shakes his head. "You have twenty-four hours to make a decision. Work for me, or your next fix will be laced with so much fentanyl, all the Narcan in the world won't save your ass."

The video keeps going as Veronica runs out of the abandoned mall, though she's moving too quickly to see anything but a blur. Mitzi screams, and the phone swings up with a split-second view of the terror in Veronica's eyes before the recording shuts off.

"Oh God," Isabel whispers and buries her face in her hands. "She was so scared..."

"She's safe, darlin'. Remember that." Shit. I never would have brought Isabel with me if she weren't so worried about having enough time to fix her grant proposal. The other two videos? From the quick glance I took at them on the way in from the truck, Veronica managed to record a quick shot of Mitzi tied up in the corner of the sporting goods shop *and* a thirty-second clip of Boswell chasing after her.

"Connor," Brent says, his voice taking on a tone that tells me I'm not going to like what comes next. "The video will go a long way to makin' sure Boswell never breathes free air again. But that doesn't change the Bureau's stance on the case. I can't help you."

"Goddamnit, Brent. I've given the FBI almost twenty years of my life!" I slam my fist down on the table hard enough to rattle his fork on the plate. "And you can't do this *one* thing for me? I'm not askin' for a whole task force. Two agents. Maybe three. Captain Stone's unit is stretched thin, and we still don't know if the corruption in the police department extends beyond Milton and Archer."

Brent stares me down like I'm four quarters short of a dollar. With both his hands flat on the table, he leans in and lowers his voice. "Twenty years and you still think the rules don't apply to you. If I ignore protocol on this, my ass will be shitcanned right along with yours. I *should* demand you turn over your credentials and your firearm right fucking now, but instead, I'm givin' you until the end of next week to put in your retirement papers so you can get your pension. Until then, I don't want to hear a goddamn word about this investigation. You have resources. Ones I cannot know about. Officially, we never met up today, you never showed me that video, and I *definitely* didn't tell you to call the man who saved your life and get his help instead."

"Put in your retirement papers..."

For a long moment, I hold his gaze, too shocked to say a word. Until Isabel's hand rests on my thigh and she squeezes gently.

"Right. We're goin'." Swiping the phone off the table, I slide out of the booth and help Isabel to her feet. "This isn't what I wanted, Brent. I hope you know that."

He doesn't look up. Just shakes his head and sighs. "Don't make no never mind. Because you were never here."

***

Isabel

The drive to my office passes in silence. Connor holds on to the steering wheel so tightly, his knuckles are almost white, and a vein at his temple throbs at regular intervals. I wish I knew what to say to him, but I think his boss just fired him—in a way—and it's all my fault. So I stay quiet.

At the elevator, I pause to dig out my keycard, and Connor puts his back to mine—scanning the parking garage, I assume—until the doors whisper open. When I turn around, he's still on alert, his hand hovering over the butt of his gun until we're safely on the way to the tenth floor.

"No one expects me to be here today. It's Sunday. If we see anyone—except maybe Luke—I'll be shocked."

"Not takin' any chances." His words are clipped, harsh, and I reach for his arm, but he stiffens and pulls away. "No chances means I need to have both hands free, Isabel."

Isabel? Not darlin'? And with that tone? Oh, hell no.

Hands on my hips, I peer up at him. "Listen here, stud. I get that you're pissed at your boss. But—"

"Former boss."

That earns him an eye roll. "Fine. Former boss. Don't interrupt me. You've been nothin' but the perfect gentleman since the day we met. But right now, you're makin' a hornet look cuddly."

Connor flinches like I just slapped him and sucks in a slow, deep breath. But before he can reply, the elevator dings, and the doors slide open.

"Come on, then. My office is at the end of the hall." Hiking my purse strap higher on my shoulder, I start walking, not waiting for him to "clear the space" or get ahead of me.

He doesn't try to touch me or say a word until we're in my office, but less than two seconds after Connor locks the door, he's on me, backing me against the wall with his hands on my hips and raw emotion churning in his eyes. "I don't know who I am if I'm not an FBI agent."

"You're Connor Davis. Quinton's brother. Your mama's son. Veronica's protector and bringer of BBQ and burgers. And you're the man I'm perilously close to falling in love with. When you're not actin' so ornery you can't see straight."

After a beat, he crushes his mouth to mine. The kiss takes me by surprise, and he pins me with his bulk. The bold strokes of his tongue make me his in every way until he pulls back, his eyes shining. "I don't deserve you, darlin'."

"You deserve love, Connor. And I'll have words with anyone —including you—who tries to convince me otherwise."

I lose myself in his gaze, time standing still until I step off the edge of the precipice and let myself fall. I should be scared.

I loved once, and when Tony died, I built a wall around my heart so tall and so strong, I didn't think it would ever crumble. But Connor broke through, and when I cup his cheek, he covers my hand with his.

"If we were somewhere I knew was safe...somewhere we could be alone for a good long time, I'd show you just how hard I've fallen—and I'd say the words that have been knockin' around in my head since this mornin'. But I want you all to myself when I do. So grab what you need and let's get out of here."

I shove my laptop and power supply into the briefcase I left under my desk, slide the thick file folder with copies of all the grant paperwork in next to it, and retrieve my keycard from my purse. "Ready—"

Connor plucks the card from my hand and stares at it. "This...is your building access card?"

"Yes... Why? You're scaring me, Connor."

"Fuck. *Fuck!* We need to get the hell out of here, Isabel. Right now. Take the card and stay behind me." He pulls his gun from the holster on his belt, ratchets the slide, and then presses his ear to the door.

"This is ridiculous. No one's here today. The parking garage was practically empty."

Spinning around, he cups the back of my neck with his free hand and holds me still. "I found part of a card just like this where Boswell had Mitzi and Veronica. Someone from Second Chances is a part of this."

"Oh, God. That's...that's how Reggie figured out who to target." Panic swirls in my belly, and my heart hammers against my chest. "The sober living home... The director was certain more than two thirds of the men and women we'd sent to her over the past six months had relapsed, but our records said otherwise. Because they were tampered with. We have to find out who it is."

"What we have to do is *leave*. Get back to the safehouse and call for reinforcements. Everything else can wait." Connor flips the lock, cracks the door, and glances down the hall. "Clear. Stay close."

We rush toward the elevator, my laptop bag banging against my hip. I swipe the access card against the security sensor, and the car chimes seconds later.

"As soon as I unlock the truck, you climb in from the driver's side and get down. All the way to the floorboards, Isabel. And you don't get up until I say it's safe."

I don't believe anyone would come after me here. Or...at all. *I* can't identify Reggie Boswell. Or that other cop, Archer. But Connor is convinced we're in danger, and though I hope he's overreacting, I trust him enough to do what he says.

The doors slide open, and Connor sweeps his gaze from one side of the garage to the other. "Get ready," he hisses, and I clutch the laptop bag and my purse to my chest.

We're halfway to the truck when a loud crack makes my ears ring. My left shoulder burns, and my purse hits the ground, wallet, keys, lipstick, and tissues tumbling free.

"Isabel!" Connor jumps in front of me, aiming to my left and firing twice in rapid succession.

"Danny's down!" a male voice shouts from behind us. "Kill the big one, but keep the woman alive!"

Warmth trickles down my arm, and between the burning pain and the coppery scent of blood, it hits me. I've been *shot!* Before panic can steal what's left of my faculties, Connor grabs my hand and tugs me behind a pillar. "I counted four of them. Plus 'Danny,' who's no longer a threat. When I tell you to run, you head for the truck as fast as you can. Leave the laptop."

"But—"

"Leave it, darlin'. It ain't worth your life."

My life. And Connor's. *Kill the big one.*

I nod, and Connor presses the truck keys into my hand. "If

I'm not *right* behind you, drive like a prairie fire with a tail wind. Get yourself somewhere with a fuckton of people, and call AJ's office."

"Without you? No. I can't!"

A whisper—too quiet to make out the words—comes from somewhere to our right, and Connor spins around, the gun held tight in both hands. "Go!"

I don't think. Just run.

It's so loud. So many shots. Connor's gun. At least two others. Concrete shards explode from just in front of me, and I stumble, catching myself when a familiar voice calls my name.

"Stop right there, babe." Luke steps out from behind Connor's truck with a gun pointed at my shoulder. "I don't *want* to hurt you, but I will. Tell me where Veronica is."

"You'll have to kill me!" My daughter's life is worth ten of mine, and I can see it in Luke's eyes. He knows I'll never give her up. Adjusting his grip on the gun, he smiles, and Connor screams my name a split second before Luke squeezes the trigger.

The shot whizzes by my ear—close enough I can feel the stir of the air—and when I turn, Connor crumples to the ground, blood streaming from his temple.

My skull explodes in pain, and tears burn my eyes. "Connor..."

Voices surround me, the shadows closing in, stealing the light until I can't tell where I am anymore. I'm falling, and the man I love isn't here to catch me. But the real agony? Knowing I'm leaving my daughter all alone.

CHAPTER NINETEEN

Isabel

My fingers are numb. Lifting my head is too hard, and I groan softly. The sound echoes. I try to move my arms, but something hard digs into my wrists as metal clinks close to my ear.

Where am I? Nothing smells right. Feels right. The air is musty and stale, the floor smooth under my cheek.

The ambush. Luke with a gun. Connor's shout. Then the shot. He wasn't moving. All that blood. A sob tears from my throat, and the effort makes the hammer currently pounding against my skull beat a thousand times harder. He's dead... because of me.

Everything's blurry, and I blink hard several times until the swirls of the marble floor tiles come into focus. Movement in my periphery makes me whimper, and I try to shrink back, but everything starts to spin, and I let myself go limp.

"Mrs. Lopez?"

Mitzi? Oh, God. I'm with Mitzi.

Slowly, carefully, I turn my head towards the sound of her voice. Her hands are cuffed to bars that run from the floor to the ceiling, and I'm so confused until she whispers, "We're in an old bank vault. Don't scream. Please. If Reggie hears you, it'll be bad."

Shit. She's shaking, but wraps her hands around the cuffs so they don't rattle. A bruise darkens her right eye, clearly from more than two days ago since it's already turning a sickly yellow. Fast food wrappers and crumpled drink containers surround her, and her peach Austin Academy sweatshirt is stained with dirt and a few drops of blood.

Beyond the bars, a large, circular door is partly open, and a single shaft of sunlight spills in. The walls I can see are nothing but safe deposit boxes, all locked, and recessed lights in the ceiling chase the shadows away.

"Are you okay?" I ask, trying to keep my voice as low as possible. "Did they hurt you?"

She shakes her head. "Is V safe? Reggie won't stop looking for her, Mrs. Lopez. And he'll kill all of us once he has her. He comes a couple of times a day and asks me where else to look, and I can't...he'll make you tell him..."

"Shhh. He won't, sweetheart. I'll die before I tell him where she is. But...we have to find a way out of here."

The room isn't spinning as badly as it was, so I wriggle until I can press my hands to the marble floor and push myself to sitting. Mitzi's all the way in the opposite corner of the vault—a good twenty feet away—so I can't wrap my arms around her and tell her it'll all be okay.

Not that it will. The cuffs are so tight, they dig into my wrists, and I hear voices outside—too far away to make out what they're saying. We're trapped here.

I counted four of them.

And that didn't include Luke. So five men, at least. Maybe six, since I doubt Reggie would have risked his own life to get me.

Find something you can use as a weapon.

My keys were in my purse. I'm not wearing any jewelry other than the tiny gold hoops I never take off. I'm still fully clothed—thank God—but my pockets are empty.

Mitzi stares past me, her eyes widening. "He's moving! I thought he was dead."

He?

Connor!

A soft, muffled groan has my heart leaping into my throat, and I scramble to turn around. "Connor, thank God." He's against the wall, eyes closed, his wrists locked to the last bar in the room. Blood covers the whole left side of his face, still tacky and glistening. Trails of crimson snake across his forehead, down his nose, and into his eyes. He's close enough I can stretch my leg out and nudge his hip with my foot. "Wake up, stud. I need you. *We* need you."

He jerks his hands, and the cuffs rattle loudly. "Wh —Fuuuuuuuck."

"Connor? Open your eyes. Please..."

"Head..." he murmurs. The muscles of his neck cord and strain with the effort of moving even an inch, and it takes him half a dozen tries before he can rake his fingers over the blood covering his lids. One eye opens to a slit, then almost immediately closes. "Isa..."

"I'm right here." Rubbing small circles on his thigh, I strain to close some of the distance between us, but the handcuffs dig into my wrists and I stifle my whimper. "I can't get any closer, but you can. At least a little. Come on, stud. Show me what you're made of."

From the pain etched in the lines around his lips, it takes everything he has to open his eyes and focus on me. "Can't... words...ev'thing...fuzzy."

Fuzzy? His head.

"Woke up in the hospital unable to walk, talk, or think..."

I've never wanted to hurt someone as badly as I want to hurt Luke in this moment.

The man I love—I know it now, I'm absolutely, completely, hopelessly in love with Connor—isn't the man in front of me. What if he's gone forever? I'll still love him for as long as I live. Even if that's only another few hours. But in his current state, will he understand if I tell him how I feel?

It's agonizing to watch him struggle to move. But after a minute, he wraps his fingers around one of the bars and pulls himself up an inch at a time until he's leaning against the wall.

"How...long...?" Wincing when he opens his eyes again, he turns his head away, then feels along his hairline until his fingers reach the deep gash at his temple.

"I don't know." I glance back at Mitzi. "When did they bring us in here?"

"Dunno. Maybe ten minutes before you woke up?"

Connor yanks at the cuffs, suddenly agitated enough I'm worried he's going to hurt himself. "Who's...?"

"It's Mitzi. Calm down. Please. We have to stay quiet." Behind me, Mitzi starts to cry. I wish I could scream. Wail. Let myself shatter into a million pieces, but I can't. My daughter's best friend and the man I love need me, and if I fall apart now, what will happen to Veronica?

"Connor? Can you move? Come any closer? I..." Shit. It doesn't matter that I want his arms around me. The distance between us is too great. No matter how much he stretches, I can't hold him. Can't cup his cheek or feel his heartbeat. "Wait," I say when he lifts his head and the muscles in his jaw tense. "Save your strength. Rest."

"Uh huh," he mumbles, and his head lolls onto his shoulder. This time, when my eyes burn, I don't try to stop the tears from tumbling down my cheeks. We're going to die here, and I pray Veronica's still safe.

THE VOICES from outside the vault come and go, sometimes angry, sometimes not. With no other way to mark the passage of time, I watch the tiny patch of sunlight move across the floor until it fades away. It must be at least six, and we left my office a little after one. Connor stirs occasionally, shifts his position, but he hasn't opened his eyes again. At least the bleeding has stopped. I think.

A door slams, and he jerks awake, looking around wildly until his gaze locks with mine.

"About fucking time," a gritty male voice snaps.

Mitzi lets out a sob. "No, no, no," she whispers.

"What is it?" I hiss, and from the fear in her red-rimmed eyes, I know. Reggie.

"Let me go, shithead!"

My world crumbles to dust at the sound of my daughter's voice. Heavy footsteps thud closer, and another man growls, "I should drop you right now, you little bitch."

"Don't talk to her that way!" I scream, pulling on the chain until the bars rattle and blood seeps from under the cuffs. I can't stand up. Not fully. The vertical bars are bisected by three horizontal ones, but I get to my knees just as Archer—the detective Veronica said was the one who grabbed Mitzi—strides in with my baby girl thrown over his shoulder.

She pounds on his back with her good hand and tries to kick him, but he has her legs pinned tight against his chest. As soon as he's fully inside the vault, he dumps her onto the floor, and her thin, pained whimper sends me over the edge.

"You fucking animal. I'll kill you!" My wrists are slick with blood, and the pain sends sparks of electricity running up my arms. Hunched over, I scream and rage and use all my strength to try to get free. I don't care how much it hurts. Nothing matters more than clawing Archer's eyes out before I bang his head into the bars over and over.

A fist slams into my cheek so hard, I see stars. Connor roars —or is that my heartbeat in my ears?—and I fall to my knees. Someone grabs me by the hair and yanks my head back.

Reggie sneers down at me. This close, the look in his eyes is so vile, it makes my blood run cold. "I'd kill you right now, bitch, but I still need you and your daughter. The blond one? She's served her purpose. Tell me what I need to know, and I'll make all your deaths quick and painless. One bullet to the back of the head. Fight me, and I'll make it last for days."

Mitzi and Veronica are both crying now, and Archer has Connor pinned to the ground, his boot planted firmly in the center of Connor's chest.

We're all dead. The fight drains from my body in an instant. When Reggie loosens his grip on my hair, I collapse. "Much better." Cutting his gaze to Archer, he jerks his thumb at Veronica, who dragged herself over to Mitzi. The two girls hug one another, both sobbing, until Archer wraps a meaty hand around Veronica's arm.

"No!" she shrieks, but he's too strong. In under a minute, he's zip tied her good wrist to one of the bars and has her ankles bound with a second, thicker tie.

"Please, don't do this," I beg, forcing the words out over my terror. "She's just a kid..."

The look Reggie gives me is pure hatred. "She's a fucking pain in the ass. I had to kill the bitch I was grooming because of her. Milton and Archer are practically useless now, and I need to find new cops to put on the payroll. Your *kid* is going to cost me a goddamn fortune. So before I kill you, you're going to tell me what evidence she has on me and where I can find it."

He pulls out a switchblade, and the snap as it flies open makes me flinch. Waving it back and forth in a figure eight, he smiles as his cold, angry gaze bores into me. "Start talking."

CHAPTER TWENTY

Connor

"Asshole!" The single word takes all my focus. The moment I opened my eyes, I knew I was fucked. I can't remember how I ended up here. We were in the parking garage, then nothing. But between the near-constant flashes and halos obscuring my vision, the migraine dialing every sensation up to a thousand, and barely being able to speak, I'm in deep shit.

Boswell spares me only the briefest of glances—I think—before advancing on Isabel.

"Hey. Shhhh-shit...head. I'm...talking...to you." Curling my hands around the bars, I rattle them as hard as I can, and he finally takes notice.

"Shut him up," Reggie snaps, and the other sombitch, Archer, ambles over and aims a swift kick to my gut. But I'm ready for it, and while it hurts like hell, it doesn't take me down.

"Baaaaad...move." *Think. Focus. You can do this.*

Aphasia. The inability to form words. I know what I want to say—what I need to say—but the pathway between my brain and my mouth short-circuited, and there's nothing that'll fix it but time. When I woke up in the hospital months ago, struggling to communicate terrified me. And now, it's back. Worse than ever.

"W-want t'know...where...?" There's no fucking way I'll be able to make him understand. Not before he loses his patience and starts hurting Mitzi. She's expendable, and from the way she's sobbing, she knows it.

His interest is piqued, though, and he stares down at me like he can't quite figure me out. "You don't know shit, Mr. F-B-I. The only reason you're still alive is because sooner or later, that Texas Ranger in charge of huntin' me down is gonna message you, and I might need your face to unlock your phone again. Usin' your GPS to get from the apartment to the Lopez place yesterday was also damn convenient. Archer was workin' an angle to get the address, but it hadn't panned out yet."

I can *feel* Isabel staring at me, but I can't look her in the eyes. Veronica's here because of me. Billings and McGrath... they're probably dead because of me.

He's read my text messages, but he couldn't have accessed the videos or anything I got from Zephyr. Those are all encrypted with a ten-digit passcode. I thought she was off her rocker for insisting on the additional security, but now...thank fuck she did.

Boswell mutters, "Useless," under his breath and turns back to Isabel, waving that goddamn switchblade like a cape at a rodeo.

"Leave my mom alone!" Veronica cries. "She didn't do *anything* to you. *I* did!"

Isabel screams as Boswell turns toward V. That kid might be the bravest seventeen-year-old on the planet. If she's not giving up, I can't either. "Vid. Of...you, asshole," I grit out, and he freezes, the blade inches from Veronica's cheek. "Want...it?"

Archer grabs me by the throat and slams me against the

wall. One more blow to the head and I'm scared I'll be fucked. Permanently.

Swallowing bile, I force myself to breathe until Boswell orders Archer to let me go. My legs won't hold me, and I hit the ground.

"Vid? You mean video?" Reggie asks, crouching down close enough, not even the constant halos can hide the desperation in his eyes. "Where is it?"

Shit. I didn't think this through. He'll lose patience with me before I can explain, and I have no way of telling Isabel that we have to get *someone* from Boswell's crew to go to her house. Zephyr's monitoring her security system, and she can access the doorbell camera footage.

Unless...

"Tablet. Her room. Zee..." Cutting my gaze to Isabel, I pray she figures out what Z stands for.

"I can't understand anything this brain-damaged idiot says," Boswell mutters and turns to Isabel. "Explain or his head won't be the only part of him bleeding."

Tears race down her cheeks, and she shakes her head. "Veronica's tablet. It's...at the house. But the video—"

"Is on there. *She*...sent it." I dig my fingers into my palms as hard as I can. With every passing minute, the words become a little easier, and if I can just keep talking, maybe we'll have a chance. "Yesterday. I said it was safe. She could see..."

Understanding dawns in Isabel's eyes. "The video's on the tablet," she says. "But I have to be the one to get it for you. My security system goes off sometimes. If the company calls and I don't answer, they'll send a patrol."

"Archer won't be there long enough for anyone to show up," Reggie snaps. "You're not going anywhere. None of you are."

"You want them to know I'm missing?" Isabel cries as Reggie and the piece of shit detective head for the vault door.

"They'll call the Rangers. Then someone will go to the safe-house and find out Veronica's gone."

Reggie slams his hand against the bars. "Fuck!" He whirls around, drops to one knee, and presses the blade to Isabel's throat. She doesn't move. Doesn't break eye contact with him. "Milton!" he shouts. "Get in here!"

Veronica shrinks against the bars when the cop saunters in, and *if it's the last thing I do, I'm going to rip his balls off and shove them down his throat.*

"Can we kill them now?" Milton asks.

"No. You and Archer are taking the bitch to her house. Check in every ten minutes." Leaning closer to Isabel, Boswell flicks the blade along her jaw, and she hisses in pain. "If you try *anything*, I'll start carving pieces off little Mitzi one at a time."

"I won't," Isabel whispers. "But I need to hug my daughter first. And Connor."

Milton unlocks Isabel's handcuffs and Boswell yanks her to her feet. "You ask for nothing. *I'm* in charge here." He shoves her at Archer, who twists her right arm behind her back until she cries out. "Take her. And send Luke in here with Mr. FBI's cell phone. I want to make sure he doesn't have any new messages from that Ranger."

Isabel tries to lunge for her daughter, but Archer muscles her out of the vault as Veronica cries, "Mom! Don't go!"

A man in a fucking suit stops right in front of Isabel, a sheepish grin on his face. "Sorry, babe. It wasn't my idea to go after Veronica. She just...got in the way."

Isabel doesn't stop cursing him until one of the cops—Milton, I think—tells her she can shut up or he'll make her.

As Luke saunters in, a flash of memory fans the rage burning like a wildfire inside of me. *This smug bastard is her coworker. And he's the one who shot me.*

Isabel

Two feet from the door, Milton jams his gun against my ribs hard enough to make me gasp. "This ain't like the mall. Still some folks passin' by this time of night. You make a peep and Reggie's gonna hear about it. The car's less than thirty feet away, and you and I are gettin' in the back, all nice and cozy like we're in *love*."

"No one's going to believe that," I mutter.

"Sure they will." Milton shoves the gun into his jacket and drapes his arm around my shoulders. His breath reeks of stale coffee, and my stomach pitches. "Smile, sweet cheeks."

I can't, but at least I manage not to cry as we walk—calm as can be—to a dark brown sedan. Archer opens the back door, then crowds against me while Milton slides in first. "Back off, asshole," I snap. "You have my daughter. I can't save her, but you can be damn sure I'm gonna do anything I can to make her death as painless as possible."

He shoves me, and I end up sprawled across Milton's lap. Disgusting. The door slams shut, and I scramble upright and fasten my seat belt like some kind of shield.

If I misunderstood Connor, Reggie is going to make us all suffer. How the hell is Zephyr going to find us? Even if she does, there's no way she'll be fast enough. Milton elbows me in the side when I try to get my bearings and search for a cross street, so I keep my head bowed, flicking my gaze to the clock on the dashboard at regular intervals.

If I'm lucky, I'll have two chances to get a message to Zephyr. The doorbell camera video—where I have to tell her to call my house and pretend to be my security company—and the all-too-brief phone call. There's no way these two apes will leave me alone for either one, so whatever I tell her can't be... obvious. Is there any way I can let her know we're being held in a bank? There can't be that many abandoned vaults in Austin.

Think, Isabel. There has to be something you could say.

My inner voice fights me the whole trip, and with every turn, every stop light, every street we pass, I lose more of the scant hope Connor gave me.

After exactly ten minutes, Milton texts Reggie, and at eighteen, Archer pulls into my driveway.

Dangling my keys in front of me, Milton grins. "Remember, sweet cheeks. We're in love."

"You disgust me." I snatch the keys out of his hand and shove them into my pocket as Archer opens the back door. "Y'all keep your damn hands to yourselves." I'm out of the car and up the steps before either of them can touch me, my right sleeve tugged up enough my bloody wrist should be visible on the doorbell camera. With any luck, the crimson staining my shoulder will register too.

"I have to disarm the security system," I say, letting my hand shake so much, I have trouble getting the key into the lock. "The company will probably call in under five minutes. The landline is in the kitchen. When it rings, *I* need to be the one to answer it. They're gonna ask me to confirm there's no emergency and I'll have to give them my codeword."

Milton elbows me out of the way, takes the keys, and opens the door. "Try anything, bitch, and—"

"I *know*," I say, staring right into the doorbell camera. "Reggie will hurt Veronica. And Mitzi. And Connor. You don't have to keep reminding me we're all gonna die. You think I could forget that? Her tablet with the video of you and Reggie is in her room."

Despite how terrified I am, how much I wish I were with Veronica right now, I move calmly to the security system's keypad and punch in my ten-digit code.

Archer heads down the hall to Veronica's room while Milton—after he texts Reggie—wraps his fingers around my bicep and steers me into the kitchen. I'm about to tell him to let me go when the phone rings and I stifle my yelp.

"I'm listenin' in," Milton growls, right in my ear.

Shit. Please, Zephyr. Don't go off script.

"Hello?"

"Is this Isabel Lopez?" Zephyr's voice takes on a bored tone after I confirm my identity. "We received an alert from your security system, ma'am. Can you confirm you're safe and there's no emergency?"

"I can. This happens all the time. I swear, some days it goes off when I'm twenty minutes from home."

"I need your code word, ma'am."

I went through a hundred different options on the way here. Ninety-nine of them were so ridiculous, Milton would call Reggie instantly. The only chance I have is to get Zephyr to focus on Connor. Tracing a cell phone's location is a thing, I think. "Quinton."

At my side, Milton frowns, but Zephyr clears her throat. "Thank you, ma'am. That's confirmed. Is there anything else I can do for you today?"

She wants me to give her more. Oh, God. There isn't anything else I can say.

My hesitation tries Milton's patience, and he presses the barrel of his gun to my temple and mouths, "*Hang up. Now.*"

"N-no. But tell your boss I need this problem fixed as soon as possible. All these calls are going to be the death of me."

Milton snatches the phone out of my hand with a muttered curse and drops it on the floor where it shatters into a dozen pieces. "We're leaving. Archer? You got the tablet?"

"Right here," he says, holding it up as he saunters down the hall. "What's the password?"

"I don't know. It's my daughter's. I don't spy on her. Only she can unlock it. We have to go back." If they check the tablet now, they'll figure out there's no video, and start in on Mitzi. Probably Connor too. Zephyr needs time to find us. But...I couldn't give her what she needed. She knows Quinton is Connor's brother, but what good is that going to do?

Only Milton's arm around my shoulders keeps me from collapsing on the way back to the sedan. My tears won't stop, and once Archer pulls out of my driveway, I let myself fall apart. My sobs fill the car, and no matter how many times Milton tells me to stop, I can't. It doesn't matter if he hits me. Threatens me. Even shoots me.

When we get back to the bank, we're all going to die. Because I failed. It's all my fault. I won't fire the gun, but Veronica? Connor? Mitzi? I'll be the one who kills them.

CHAPTER TWENTY-ONE

Connor

I FAILED. I couldn't protect Isabel or Veronica. They used *my* phone to find the kid. To kill Billings and McGrath. And soon? We'll join them.

Quinton will never know what happened to me. Our mama...she'll be all alone. No. My brother will move her out to Seattle. Once he figures out I'm gone. He'll take care of her. But I won't get to tell him how proud I am of him. How much I love him. How sorry I am that I pushed him away for years.

Luke—the smug motherfucker—wasn't gentle when he shoved my head back so my phone would unlock. I didn't fight him. No point. I've barely moved since they took Isabel. He knows I'm not a threat. Even if I weren't handcuffed to these damn bars, I doubt I could take him. Not now. The migraine rages, making the world too loud, too bright, too...*everything*. So I close my eyes and conserve my strength.

After a few minutes, Reggie's footsteps recede, and not long after, Luke kicks my calf—hard. When I don't react, he chuckles and mutters something about me being a vegetable before he leaves the vault.

"Connor!" Veronica whispers. "Wake up! You have to get us out of here!"

I don't want to open my eyes, but I have to. I might not be able to save the girls, but I won't let them think they're alone.

Meeting her gaze, I hold up my cuffed hands. They took my gun, my multi-tool, and my keys when they brought us here. Even my belt. I'm shocked they left my boots on. "Awake. Can't fight...like this," I say. At least my words are coming easier now, but talking is still an effort. "Head messed up. No...weapons."

Veronica shoves her fingers into her cast, and after a full minute of wriggling, her face contorted in pain, she pulls out a stainless steel kitchen fork at least ten inches long. "Will this help?"

Holy shit. The kid had that up her arm this whole time? Angling a glance out the door, I wince. Reggie and Luke are too close. Their voices carry, though I can't make out what they're saying. They'd hear a metal fork sliding across the floor. "Too loud."

"Not if you catch it."

"V. Look...at me. Talking...is hard enough."

She tucks the fork up her other sleeve and *signs, "No talk."*

Shit.

The aphasia doesn't stop me from communicating. I can write, type, or sign without issue. This could work. It's not easy with my hands cuffed so close together, but I fumble through finger-spelling the words I don't know. *"Bags. Behind you. Wrap it up."*

Veronica motions for Mitzi to slide a couple of the bags over to her, and despite her good hand being zip-tied to one of the bars, she manages to get multiple layers of paper around the fork, then slides it across the marble tiles until it hits my leg.

"What was that?" Reggie asks. "Check on the brats."

I shove the bag behind me and drop my head. Luke's voice is too close, but all he does is snap at the girls to stay quiet and walk away. A minute later, I strain to hear his words. "Lover boy is passed out, and the kids are too scared to do more than cry. No one's gonna hear them—even if they scream."

"Whatever. In half an hour, we'll have the video the kid recorded. Break a couple of the blond one's fingers and the others will tell us if they shared it with anyone."

Their voices fade away, and I blow out a long, slow breath. Maybe I *can* do this. Get out of these cuffs, free the girls, and somehow find a way to save Isabel too.

Mitzi curls into a ball in the corner, her entire body shaking as she sobs. "I don't want to die. My mom...I want my mom..."

"Mitz? Look at me," Veronica says, her voice taking on a harsh edge even though she's still whispering. "Connor's a badass. And my mom's smart. They'll figure something out. I know it. We're gonna be okay."

I wish I had the kid's confidence instead of just a kitchen utensil.

That's not all you have, dumbass. Twenty years of training. Something to fight for. The woman you love, her daughter, and her best friend. Stop feeling sorry for yourself and get out of the damn cuffs.

The pounding in my head intensifies as I struggle to wedge the fork tines between the links on the handcuff chain. The things are so small, it's damn near impossible. But after a few minutes, the chain snaps, and my hands are free.

My arms ache from so long in one position, but time is running out. If I don't get the girls free soon, Archer and Milton will be back with Isabel and Veronica's tablet. If Zephyr wasn't at her computer, if she doesn't check the doorbell camera footage, we're fucked. Hell, we're probably fucked anyway, but Pritchard and his guys—along with AJ and Jasper—found me in the middle of nowhere, in a search area the size of New York

City. I have to believe there's a chance. Even if there isn't, I ain't going down without a fight.

The moment I get to my knees, the vault starts to spin. *Focus. Deep breaths.*

The only thing going for me? I've been through this before. Pushing through the effects of a concussion? Not smart. Not easy. For all I know, I have a brain bleed that'll take me out in minutes. But as long as I can string two thoughts together, I'll fight.

I stagger over to Veronica, one shaky step at a time, until I can kneel next to her. I don't expect her to throw her broken arm around me, and it almost knocks me onto my ass, but she holds on tight enough to steady me. "The Rangers are dead. I screamed as loud as I could, but...it was so fast. Like...two minutes and they had me in the back of a van. Archer...hit me, and everything went fuzzy."

"Shhh, lil'...bit." If we had time, I'd try to reassure her, but it's already been at least fifteen or twenty minutes since they left with Isabel, and I have no fucking clue how far we are from her house. Drawing back, I wedge the fork tines around the zip tie at her ankles and snap it in two. Then break the one securing her wrist.

I gesture for her to take the fork and free Mitzi. Holding onto the bars, I stifle my grunt as I pull myself to standing. My equilibrium goes to shit, and I tighten my grip until the world stops spinning so badly. The snap of the handcuff chain helps me focus, and I try a step. I must have wrenched my knee when I fell at some point, but the pain? It can be ignored. As long as I don't topple over, don't get a halo so bad I can't see a damn thing, I can do this.

One glance around the vault door bolsters my confidence. No one's in the bank lobby. Only the emergency lights are on out there, and a long bank of teller windows stretch across the space. The glass in them? Most likely bulletproof.

Directly beyond the vault door, a narrow hallway runs for a good twenty feet to the right, and maybe forty on the left before continuing at a ninety-degree angle. That's the way they took Isabel. I could hear the echoes as she cussed a blue streak at Milton.

Three doors probably hide offices. Only one—the middle door—is open, and light spills into the hall, broken up by shadows moving every few seconds.

"They're ten minutes out," Reggie says, but whatever Luke says in reply is too muffled for me to hear.

Fuck. We're running out of time. I retreat, dropping down next to Veronica and Mitzi. My ASL is rusty, but I manage to ask V if she could remember anything from when they brought her here.

"The door is down the hall to the left. There's a parking lot, but I think it's behind the bank, because I couldn't see anyone around. Just the street lights. We passed an office...maybe a couple, but only one had a light on. It was messy, and the guy in the suit was at a desk with his feet up."

"You are...wow," I sign, and the look she gives me? Shit. For a second, she beams like she just climbed Mt. Everest. *"Walk?"*

"They took my leg brace in the van," V says. "But I can try."

Mitzi sits up a little straighter. "She can lean on me."

These girls are so fucking brave, they make me believe we have a chance. But now comes the hard part. I hope to all that's holy I can get the words I need out of my broken brain, because signing? It'll take too damn long.

"I keep watch. You go to front doors. Out. Then right. Don't stop. Find a crowd. Only call the Rangers. No police. Don't let... anyone...call the police."

"What about Mom?" Veronica asks.

"Won't leave without her. Promise." I might not leave at all, but the girls don't need to know that.

Holding out her hand, Veronica offers me her little finger. Fuck me. I broke our last pinky swear. I couldn't protect Isabel at her office. *I* let her be taken. Let myself get shot. If I'd moved quicker...if I'd shown her the piece of plastic before sending it to Zephyr...if I'd paid more attention when she used it the first time...

Seeing the woman I love in pain, bleeding, desperate to protect her daughter? It nearly killed me. I can't fail again. As long as the girls are safe, I don't care what happens to me.

"She's my whole world, Connor. Almost everything good in my life is tied to her."

My hand shakes, but I hook my pinky around Veronica's and squeeze lightly. "Get ready to run."

Before I can grab the bars and pull myself up, Veronica throws her arms around me and whispers in my ear. "If you don't kick their asses, I'll hate you forever, Connor. And since you're in love with my mom, that's gonna make the rest of your life *really* difficult."

I'm so shocked, I can't respond until she and Mitzi are standing at the vault door waiting for me to get my shit together. "Lil' bit," I manage, my voice rough. "If I don't make it...need you to know somethin'."

Her lower lip wobbles until she sucks it between her teeth and nods.

"You are brave as fuck. Never thought..." A flash of light blinds me, and I sway, only my grip on the bars keeping me upright. *Focus. You're running out of time.* "Never thought I'd want a kid in my life. Till I met you."

Tears shimmer in her eyes. "Never wanted a step-dad. Till I met *you*. Don't die."

I can't fail her. Can't fail Isabel. My body wants to give up. To escape the constant agony thrumming through my head and just...let go. But I've never quit a damn thing since the day I learned to walk—or so my mama used to say—and I ain't gonna start now. Not with this young woman looking at me like we're family.

Giving Veronica's shoulder a quick squeeze, I angle a glance around the vault door. The girls will only be visible for a second. Maybe two if they move fast enough. "As soon as I'm up...you go."

For the first time in my life, I'm grateful for the Bureau's physical fitness requirements. Weeks of pull-ups pay off, and I stretch out along the top of the three-foot-thick door, the long kitchen fork clamped between my teeth.

At my nod, the girls rush across the hall. So far so good. Around the teller windows. To the doors.

Mitzi pushes on the handle, hard, but it doesn't budge.

Goddammit!

She tries again, harder this time. The rattling carries, and Reggie snaps, "What the fuck is that? Find out!"

Veronica glances back at me. Even from fifty feet away, I know she's terrified. After a beat, she sweeps her gaze around the room, then points to one of the desks. The next second, she and Mitzi drop down, hidden from view by the long counter.

Turning my head so my voice *should* echo off the back wall of the vault, I shout, "Hey, asshole!" as soon as I hear the smug bastard's footsteps. "Get the fuck in here! I got things to say."

Luke stops, pokes his head back into the office, and whines, "Can I kill him now?"

"No. But you can shoot him in the kneecaps. That'll shut him up."

Fucker. I'm gonna wipe that shit-eating grin right off your ugly mug.

He's so happy Reggie told him to shoot me, he actually *spins his gun* around his finger like some cocky Wild West cowboy. Until he's faced with an empty vault.

Launching myself from the top of the door, I tackle him, clamping a hand over his mouth and taking him to the ground before he can alert Reggie. The gun slips from his hand, but the impact jars me enough, the fork hits the tiles with a loud clatter.

No longer caring about silence, I roll to my left and snag the sharp utensil as Luke shouts, "Reggie!"

The idiot lunges for the gun, completely ignoring me. Big mistake. Fisting the collar of his shirt, I yank him backward. He flails, tries to slam his head into mine, but he doesn't have my training.

The gurgle as the tines rip through his throat? Like angels singing. He'll bleed out in seconds. The room starts to spin, so I drop him. Shit. I can't pass out. Not now. I need that gun.

I manage to shove the fork into my boot, but can't find the damn pistol. Shit. A fresh halo bursts in my field of view. After a hard blink, it fades, and I see the butt of the gun poking out from *under* Luke's body.

Before I can snag it, a shot reverberates off the metal walls, and bits of marble fly up from the floor inches away, at least a few of them slicing my palm.

"I changed my mind," Reggie says as he aims higher—right at my head. "You're more trouble than you're worth."

I'm dead. There's no chance of him missing me at this range.

I was too broken, Isabel. Too slow. I tried to save her. I wish I'd said the words. I wish you knew how much I loved you.

"Do it." I close my eyes and take one last, deep breath. Don't want to see it coming. My life ain't worth shit without Isabel and Veronica. But it's better this way. Isn't it? They won't have to watch me die.

Reggie cocks the hammer, and I offer up one final prayer.

Please. I need a miracle.

Isabel. Her voice rings out like a whole choir of angels. I open my eyes, and Reggie's aim wavers. Just an inch. Is it enough? Only one way to find out.

CHAPTER TWENTY-TWO

Isabel

Milton shoves me through the door, and I hit the opposite wall. Pain zings down my arm. If looks could kill, he'd drop dead on the spot. Then again, if they could, we'd all be home. Safe. Free.

"Was that really necessary, asshole?"

"Consider it payback for getting me fired," he says with a shrug. "I've been living in cheap motels for five days now. All because of your fucking kid."

"Don't you insult her—" A loud *crack* sounds from deep inside the bank. "Veronica!"

I don't care if Milton shoots me. I have to get to my daughter. I take off at a dead run. Steps from the vault door, Milton shouts, "Boss!"

Another *crack*, this one so much louder, is followed by a muffled *"oof."*

The sight as I burst into the room steals my breath. Connor pins Reggie with his bulk, but the drug dealer punches him in the temple—right where Luke shot him. With a groan, Connor collapses onto Luke's body. His *dead* body. Oh, God. There's so much blood.

Veronica and Mitzi. Where are Veronica and Mitzi? For a split second, I'm frozen. Connor needs help. But I have to find my daughter. Have to try to get her out of here.

I only make it a single step before an arm wraps around my throat, and Milton's foul breath makes me gag. "Not so fast." Spittle hits my cheek, and I squirm and claw at him, but he's wearing a dirty sport coat, and my short nails do nothing.

Reggie scrambles to his feet, his chest heaving with each breath. "Archer! Find the brats. They're still here somewhere! And you! Mr. F-B-I. On your feet. Back against the wall, hands in the air."

From his position—one hand braced on Luke's bloody chest, Connor meets my gaze. "Isabel...I tried..."

The agony in his voice makes my heart ache. "I love you." I can't do more than whisper with Milton half choking me, but we're going to die. He has to know how I feel about him. That I know he'd do anything if it meant Veronica and I would live. "I wish we had more time..."

"Cover him," Reggie snaps. He grabs my arm and pulls me in front of him, pressing the gun against my ribs.

Connor tries to get up, but his right leg buckles, and he collapses behind Luke's body. "Need...a second," he says, his words thick and slow. "Fucked with...my head."

Leaning in, Reggie runs his nose along my cheek, then shifts, grabbing my breast and squeezing hard enough, I yelp. "Maybe you and I can have a little fun before I kill you."

"Touch her like that again, and I'll rip your dick off," Connor growls. He sways slightly on his feet, but rage shines in his eyes, so bright, they're like twin flames ready to burn down the world. And his voice? Razor sharp, and clear as a summer sky.

"You'll be dead before you take two steps." Reggie drags me

to the vault door. "Want to hear your mommy scream, Veronica? Keep hiding."

"V, don't listen—" The gun slams into my jaw, and my legs threaten to give out, but Reggie jerks me harder against him.

"Stop!" My daughter's head pops up beyond the teller windows. "Leave my mom alone!"

"Where's your friend?" Archer asks, striding across the room, grabbing the back of Veronica's neck, and steering her toward the vault. My baby girl winces with every step, but she throws her shoulders back and shakes off his hold.

"Mitzi got out. She's probably called the Rangers by now," V says with a sweet smile. Archer mutters a string of expletives and shoves her up against the bars. "I bet they'll be here any minute."

I'm so focused on Veronica, so convinced we're seconds away from dying, I don't fight when Reggie forces me to my knees in front of him. Or when he presses the barrel of the gun to the back of my head.

"Just let us go," I beg. "You have the tablet. The video. No one's seen it but us. We were going to send it to the Ranger captain once we got back from my office, but you got to us first. We can say we never saw your face."

Across from me, Connor lowers his hands. His gaze pings between me and the floor more than once, but then turns to Milton. "You and Archer? You're useless to him now. We could never get a solid ID on Boswell, but the two of you?" He snorts. "How long you think he's gonna keep you around? Your whole operation is dead in the water. No more inside man at Second Chances. No new *targets* to exploit. Y'all are fucked six ways from Sunday."

Milton glances at Reggie, and in my periphery, Archer lowers his gun slightly.

"Let Veronica go," Connor says. "And you can walk out of

here. But decide quickly, or you won't be walkin' anywhere ever again. "

"Don't fucking move," Reggie orders. "I *own* you here shitheads. All the women you've *disposed of* over the last five years? I know where you buried every one of them. And what about that cop out in Mountain City? You know what happens to cop killers in prison. One phone call from me, and the two of you are someone's bitches for the rest of your very short lives."

"Last chance, dickheads." Connor shrugs. "You think I care if you live or die?"

"Walt...?" Archer motions for Veronica to get behind him, then takes several steps *with* her toward the door. "What if he's right?"

Milton huffs. "Coward." He shoves Connor, sending him onto his ass. "Boss? Let me kill him."

"I love you, darlin'," Connor says. He rubs his leg, long, slow strokes from his knee to the top of his boot. His *good* leg. "Remember what I told you earlier? In the elevator?" His gaze drops from my eyes to the floor.

"Get down. And don't get up until I say it's safe."

He's about to do something. Something dangerous. After a quick glance around the vault, I realize I can't just stay down. Archer isn't holding a gun on my baby girl. She's not tied up. Milton's focused on Connor, and Reggie? I can *feel* his desperation. He's about to lose everything. This is the closest we've been to free since the parking garage, and I don't care if it's the last thing I do, I'm saving my daughter. And maybe, the man I love.

"Now!" Connor shouts, and I spin on my knees, grab Reggie's gun by the barrel, and twist as hard as I can.

The roar from behind me is feral. Full of rage and pain and desperation. Reggie kicks me in the stomach, and I lose my breath. The barrel slips from my grasp. In that instant, my heart crumbles into a thousand pieces. I failed. Again. And I'm going to die. Curling into a ball, I look for my daughter. As long as she's free, nothing else matters. She's out of the vault, out of Archer's reach, and she locks eyes with me.

Pushing up on an elbow, I press my hand to my heart. *"Love you, baby girl,"* I mouth.

"Mom! Get down!"

A body hits the marble to my left, and I drop seconds before Connor leaps over me and tackles Reggie. What is he holding? Silvery metal. Sharp spikes. He plunges the weapon into Reggie's chest, then wraps his fingers around the man's throat.

Despite the blood soaking into Reggie's dress shirt, he slams his gun against Connor's cheek.

Glass shatters. Shouts—lots of them—get louder by the second, and the distraction gives Connor the advantage he needs. Pulling the *thing* from Reggie's chest, he presses the twin points to the man's neck, sitting on him and pinning Reggie's arms with his knees. "Get to Veronica, darlin'. Make sure she doesn't see this."

I scramble up, only then noticing Milton crumpled in a heap, all the life gone from his eyes. Before I reach the vault door, AJ and a whole mess of Texas Rangers flood the small space. Hardison calls my name, wraps his arm around my shoulders, and guides me out into the hall where Veronica sits on the floor, Elmore at her side.

"Mom!"

My daughter and I hold onto one another, sobbing, until AJ's voice cuts through everything. "Just a few more steps. The EMTs are waiting. You're in bad shape, idiot. What the fuck were you thinking?"

"Isabel...and Veronica..."

"We're here!" I can't let my daughter go, but Connor needs me. Needs *us.*

"Mom, it's okay. I'll be right behind you," V says quietly. She swipes at her cheeks and offers me a small smile. "I'm okay. Make sure Connor is too."

Pushing through the throng of Rangers, I stop short when I see the man I love. His hazel eyes have lost all their fire. I'm not sure he can focus on me. Or anything at all. "What's wrong? Connor? Talk to me." I cup his cheeks, willing him to snap out of it, and his lips curve into a weak grin.

"Broken," he says, the word slurring a little. "Gonna get fixed up. You should come with. Veronica too. AJ? Make sure—"

"Everyone's going to the hospital." AJ gestures to the EMTs waiting in the lobby. "Mitzi's already on her way, and her mom will meet her there."

When Veronica shuffles over to us, Connor straightens, and it makes me love him even more that he'd try to be strong for my daughter. She peers up at him, tears in her eyes. "You kept your promise."

"Had to. Remember what you said earlier? 'Bout family?" he asks.

"Yeah."

Something passes between the two of them. A moment. An emotion. Whatever it is, Connor seems to draw strength from it, because he shakes off AJ's hold and stands on his own. "You mean it?"

Veronica holds out her pinky. "Yup. Promise."

He hooks his finger with hers. I don't know what they said to one another, but the meaning behind the words? Plain as day. The three of us? We're a family.

The EMTs rush over, but Connor holds on to Veronica's hand for one more moment. "Me too, lil' bit. Promise."

CHAPTER TWENTY-THREE

Connor

FOUR HOURS. It's been four hours since the EMTs loaded me into an ambulance. Four hours since the doors closed with Isabel calling my name. Four hours since I promised Veronica we'd be a family. And no one will tell me if they're okay.

The only reason I haven't gone room to room looking for them? When I tried to get up after the CT scan the docs *insisted* I have, I passed out.

Fucking concussion.

Someone stitched up the gash from the bullet—which, thank fuck didn't crack the bone—and I have a brand new brace on my knee and orders to use crutches for at least a week. Orders I'm going to ignore as soon as they let me out of here.

The door swings open, and AJ pokes his head in. "Word is, you're a stubborn son of a bitch who's not gettin' any Jell-O."

I snort, which makes the pounding in my head ten times worse. Shit.

"If you can't tell me where Isabel and Veronica are, start runnin'. Because I'm gonna kick your ass."

"Whoa! You're not running or kickin' anything for a while, dumbfuck. You had to know we were on our way. In what universe did you think it was smart to go ten rounds with those idjits?"

"The world where they were gonna kill us if I didn't do somethin'." He's trying my last nerve, and he still hasn't answered my fucking question.

"Five minutes. We were *five minutes* out when you started playing Rambo—"

"AJ..."

"They're fine," he says, holding up his hands in surrender. "Two floors down, in a room together, with Elmore and Hardison stationed outside. Damn fools refused to turn the detail over to anyone else."

A fraction of my worry eases, but it's not enough. "Care to elaborate on '*fine*'?"

"Bruises, scrapes, exhaustion. Isabel's wrists were pretty torn up, but the shoulder wound was just a graze. No stitches. The kid aggravated the knee some and caught hell for shovin' that kitchen fork down her arm until Isabel told the docs they'd all be dead if she hadn't."

My girls. Stubborn as hell and twice as smart.

Pride—and a whole mess of relief—chokes me, and all I can manage is a raspy, "Thank fuck."

AJ passes me the industrial-sized water cup, and I take a couple of sips. Wonder how much groveling I'd have to do for the nurses to put me back on the Jell-O list?

"I need to see them. Make it happen."

The Ranger's eyebrows shoot up. "You think I have that kind of power here? Shit. The nurses would laugh me right out of the building."

"Fine. I'll do it myself. If I pass out, it's on you." Shoving the blankets aside, I'm about to swing my legs over the edge of the bed when AJ grabs my shoulders and tries to push me back down.

"You're gonna want to take your hands off me right fucking now," I warn.

"You're under orders to stay in this bed. Who do you think the staff is gonna side with? Or do you want to see just how many more hits you can take before you end up with *permanent* brain damage?"

I slump back against the pillows, suddenly so tired, the idea of moving at all is too much. "You know about the aphasia." It's not a question, and shame crawls up the back of my neck.

"What do you think I've been doing for the past however long? Sitting around with my thumb up my ass? No. Been takin' statements, writin' reports, makin' sure Archer is locked up so tight, he's never seein' the light of day again...and visiting McGrath's wife."

"Fuckin' hell. I'm sorry. They were good men."

We let a moment of silence pass between us, and AJ loosens his tie. First time I've seen him anything less than a hundred percent professional.

"Some days, I really hate this job. Others...it's the only thing I live for. Today...it's both."

Before I can offer a single word of comfort, he reaches into his jacket pocket and pulls out my cell phone.

"Found it in the office the gang was using. Even charged it up for you." Dropping it into my lap, he nods and heads for the door. "You're welcome. I'll be back in an hour with Isabel and Veronica—if their docs okay it *and* they're up to it. Though Isabel's been askin' about you so much, she ain't getting Jell-O either. While I'm gone? Call your brother. He's sent me a dozen text messages since Zephyr put out the alert. Last one promised he'd be on a plane by morning if he didn't hear from you."

Quinton. When I thought I was going to die, I would have done anything to talk to him one more time. But now that we're all safe, I have no fucking clue what to say.

Just be his brother. And tell him you're sorry for all times you weren't.

My hand trembles as I dial, and when the video connects, there are tears in his eyes. "Connor..." He shakes his head and passes the phone to Graham, who wraps one arm around his shoulders and holds tight.

"I should kick your ass for what you put him through," Graham says. "But looks like someone beat me to it."

"You should see the other guy. Or not. There ain't much left of his face."

Graham's lips twitch, and Quinton swipes at his cheeks, the weariness in his expression reminding me just how much he's been through the past six months.

"I'm sorry, Q."

The nickname seems to surprise him, and I can't explain why I never used it before. He started going by Q when he escaped his ex. It's how he signs all his emails, and I never picked up on it. Never realized how such a small thing could mean so much.

"Don't apologize," he says quietly. "You love her, right? Isabel? Zephyr said you did, but I never thought you wanted..."

"A life outside the job?"

He offers me a sheepish grin. "Somethin' like that."

Just talk to him. And for fuck's sake, be honest.

"I didn't. Till I met her." I try to rake my fingers through my hair, but accidentally graze the fresh stitches above my eyebrow and let out a string of curses that shocks even Graham.

"So, you're not going back? To the FBI?" Q asks.

I can't believe how much he's changed in a few short months. His ex stole his confidence. Hell, he'd been so terrified, he couldn't take two steps beyond his front door for almost a year. Now? His shoulders don't slump. He looks me straight in the eye, and from the warning in his voice, he'll give me hell if he doesn't like my answer.

"No. As soon as I can get out of here, I'm puttin' in my retirement papers. Thought I might call Pritchard. See if he needs a washed-up relic with a permanent limp on his payroll."

"He collects them," Graham says, chuckling. "You'll fit right in. But fair warning. You're committing to at least one family holiday a year. They're a little...intense."

"Anything that involves Ryker is intense," Q adds. "He and Dax are the only people I've ever met grumpier than you, big brother. You'll fit in just fine."

Holidays. *Family* holidays.

"Connor? You look a little...green." Graham leans closer to the camera. "We'll go easy on you the first time."

"It's not that..."

Who are you kidding? It's absolutely that. And so much more.

"Worried about my future niece?" Q asks. "Because from what I hear, she's as ornery as you are."

I swallow hard, and uncertainty sits like a lead weight in my stomach.

"Never wanted a step-dad. Till now. Don't die."

"Connor? We're gonna let you get some rest." Q takes the phone from Graham, and his face fills the screen. I wish I had the words to tell him how fucking sorry I am for all the times I shut him out. "But you better call again in a couple of days. I mean it."

My finger hovers over the *End* button, but every time I blink, I'm back in that vault, knowing I'm about to die. "Q?"

"Yeah?" The hope in his tone breaks me, and I swallow hard. "I love you."

His smile sends a single tear tumbling down my cheek. "Love you too."

A WARM HAND cups my cheek, and I force my heavy lids open. Isabel. Tears glisten in her eyes. "I didn't mean to wake you."

"Come here." I need her in my arms. Need to feel her against me. To know this is real, and not some dream I'm gonna wake up from.

It takes me a couple of tries to scoot to the far side of the bed, and Isabel lies on her side, molding her body to mine. Good enough. For a while.

"You okay, darlin'?"

"Better now." She rests a hand on my chest, and I hate seeing the gauze covering her wrists. The bruises peeking out from the sleeves of the hospital robe.

"That's not an answer. What about Veronica? Where is she?" The idea of the kid all alone—despite how brave she is—doesn't sit well with me, but Isabel makes a soft shhhing sound and brushes her lips to mine.

"She practically ordered me to come see you. Then fell asleep. Elmore's in the room with her, so she won't wake up alone. We have a couple of hours."

It's not enough. But I can't ask for more. Veronica needs her mother after all of this, and until I see her for myself, there's no fucking way I'll let the two be apart for long.

"When you left," I whisper, "Veronica...you should have seen her, darlin'. I was so messed up. My head..."

"I know." She buries her face in the curve of my neck, and a single shudder runs through her before she takes a deep breath. "I wasn't sure you were going to come back to me."

"Nothin' will *ever* stop me from reachin' you, Isabel. I'd fight Satan himself if I had to. You and Veronica...you're everything to me."

We're both crying now, and I slide my fingers into her hair, holding her close until all my pent-up fear and stress eases enough for me to speak again. "Veronica saved me, Isabel. When she pulled that fork out of her cast, I about fell over."

"Wish I could have seen the look on your face. Or not, because I probably would have scolded her for picking something so sharp."

"Did you know she could sign?" Every minute Isabel spends in my arms settles another piece of my heart, even as I steel myself to be without her.

"No!" Wriggling up so we're eye to eye, she frowns. "When did she—?"

"My head was so messed up. I couldn't get the words out. Happened before, too. Aphasia. I know what I want to say, but somethin' goes wrong between my brain and my mouth. Writing, typing? Signing? I can do any of those just fine."

"You signed with her." Isabel shakes her head. "I guess I should let her learn all the swear words now. Though, who am I kidding? She probably started with those."

"Just don't go too hard on Elmore for it." Chuckling, I rub small circles on Isabel's back until all the tension in her body eases and she falls asleep in my arms.

I watch the clock, and when it hits 3:00 a.m., I know I have to let her go. Two perfect hours with the woman I love, and while I wish we'd been able to do more than hold one another, this has to be enough. For now.

"Wake up, darlin'." With a light kiss to her forehead, I breathe in her scent. Under the antiseptic, the bleach, and the hint of blood, she still smells like vanilla and lilies. Like home.

"Let me sleep a little longer," she murmurs against my neck. "Don't want to let go."

"I'd keep you right here with me forever if I could. But Veronica needs you now, and she comes first. Always."

More tears—hers and mine—and after a full twenty minutes, we finally manage to let one another go. Isabel leans down to kiss me gently—we're both so banged up, we don't dare try for anything more—then links our fingers and holds on tight.

"When you came into my life, I had no idea how much I needed you. How much I could want you in such a short time. Even before...everything, I knew what we were building was real. Special."

"I love you, darlin'. With all my heart." I'm so close to begging her to stay, but I can't let myself give in. "And Veronica...whatever she needs me to be to her, I'll be."

"She needs you to be what you already are. Her protector. Her hero. The man her mom loves. And...more. She told me what you said to her. And what she said back. So, I'll go. For now. Because we're a family now. And we're not leaving this hospital without you. Veronica's orders."

The strength of the bond between us? Between all of us? I can only choke out two words. "Yes, ma'am."

EPILOGUE

Two Weeks Later

Isabel

MY PHONE BUZZES on the counter, and after a quick check of the screen, I hurry to the door. The security system Zephyr recommended is phenomenal. Twenty-four hour video surveillance running through a company out in Seattle, biometric locks, sensors on all the windows, and at least one panic button in every room.

I press my palm to the sensor, and *three* separate locks *thunk* before I can open the door.

"Leah. How are you?" Pulling her into my arms, I try not to fall apart. Mitzi went to stay with her dad last night for the first time since...*everything*, and when the phone rang at midnight, I slipped out of bed and spent the next two hours letting her cry over FaceTime.

"Tired. But better. Mitzi called a few minutes ago. One panic attack, but she did her breathing exercises and got through it. Brian even helped."

We settle on the couch with mugs of coffee. I've missed her so much. Until last night, she hadn't been ready to see me, and more than once over the past two weeks, I've burst into tears, convinced she still blamed me for everything.

"How's...?" I wave my hand vaguely, still not sure exactly where we stand.

"Therapy's helping," she says. "Mitzi more than me, but... I'm trying. The hospital's been great. I have two more weeks before I have to work a shift, and the scheduler promised no more night shifts. I'll be home by five every day."

"I'm so glad."

"And Veronica? I know she and Mitzi talk every day, but it's so hard for Mitzi to share anything with me...I don't ask."

"Some days are better than others. She's with her therapist right now, actually. I don't know how I'm going to handle it when she goes back to school next Monday, though."

"You can call me," Leah offers. "I'll probably be a wreck, but I'll listen."

We talk for over an hour. About heavy things and nothing. And when we say our goodbyes, I know we'll be okay. Eventually.

The thing no one tells you about trauma? It's always with you. Some people ignore it. Shove the memories and the feelings down so deep, they can't see the light of day. But I tried that when I lost Tony and almost lost myself as well.

So I'm trying to listen to my emotions. To accept them. Even if sometimes, I rage and cry and scream and want to burn down the world.

Without any other distractions, I clutch my phone, staring at the screen until my eyes burn. I can do this. I can wait. Be patient. Stop myself from imagining every worst-case scenario for at least another few minutes. Can't I?

Just when I'm about to admit defeat, a gentle *ding* sets my world to rights.

On our way home. Got pizza.

My first instinct is to race into the bathroom and try to hide the evidence of all the tears I've cried today. But when I get there, I see the sticky note on the mirror in my daughter's handwriting.

No hiding.

I made a promise, and I'm going to keep it.

"Mom!" Veronica's cry pulls me from my panic attack, and I stare up at her. I'm on the floor. I don't remember how I got here. Just that we're in the hospital. That no one will tell me anything about Connor. That the MRI on her leg was supposed to be finished half an hour ago.

"Oh, God. I'm sorry, V. I..." Trying to explain only makes everything worse. I can't breathe under the crushing weight of my fear until Veronica slides down next to me.

"Tell me five things you can see. Right now, Mom." She waves the nurse away, takes my hand, and holds on tight. "Come on. You can do this."

"You," I manage. "Just you."

"Nope. Not good enough. Name five or I'm gonna tell the nurses you hate Jell-O."

I can do this. For her, I can do anything. "Bed. TV. Wheelchair. Pillow."

She takes me through the whole routine. Four things I can feel. Three things I can hear. Two things I can smell. One thing I can taste. By the time I finish, my eyes are dry.

We climb into bed together, and Veronica holds up her little finger. She hasn't asked me to pinky swear in years, but now, she waits for me to curl my finger around hers.

"When you were crying earlier? It was like after Dad died. Your

body was here, but your heart wasn't. Every time you used to hide how sad you were...I knew. You can't do that anymore."

"I promise—"

"I'm not done. You can't shut me out, and you can't sabotage this...thing...with Connor. You should have seen him, Mom. He would have died for me. For me. *And not just because I'm your daughter. Because we're family."*

How can I be this happy and this overwhelmingly sad at the same time? My seventeen-year-old daughter just went through hell, and she's comforting me. Looking out for me.

"You love him, Mom. I knew that way before tonight. And he loves you back. So promise me you won't shut him out either."

So much for not crying any more tonight. Veronica squeezes my pinky with hers, and I swipe at my cheeks with my free hand. "I promise."

The series of beeps from the front door snap me out of my memories. "Mom? Pizza's hot! Come on!"

In the kitchen, Veronica tucks a glass of pop in the crook of her arm and balances a plate loaded with not one, not two, but *three* slices of pizza on her cast. But she catches her foot on the edge of the tile, and her eyes go wide.

"Easy now, lil' bit." Connor steadies the plate—and V's arm—like it's the most natural thing in the world. For him, I think it is. He understands her. And she loves him for it.

The moment passes, the near miss already forgotten. At least in Veronica's mind. But Connor doesn't move until she's safely sitting at the table. "Hey." Winding my arms around his waist, I breathe in his scent.

"How's Leah?" he asks, leaning down so his lips brush my ear.

"Coping. Mostly." Later tonight, I'll tell him everything. Veronica too. Because we don't keep secrets in this family. Not anymore.

"What about you, darlin'? How are you?" Connor nudges my chin up, and I meet his gaze.

I want to deflect. To focus on the exhaustion in his eyes. The dark circles under them. But I made a promise. "I'm okay."

"Isabel."

"That's the truth, stud." Cupping his cheek, I offer him a smile. "I'm okay. Not good. Not bad. Just okay."

"I don't like leaving you," he says. His voice takes on a rough edge, need and desire battling in his gaze.

"I don't much care for it either. But you're home now."

Connor dips his head and kisses me. Backing me up against the counter, he holds me close, and the bulge in his Wranglers sends a thrill straight to my core.

"Get a room," Veronica says with a groan. "Or...y'know...use the one you have?"

Knowing she's feeling enough like herself to sass us? It settles something deep inside me.

"So," Connor says when we're all sitting around the table with pizza, pop, and the good napkins. "Who wants to go first tonight?"

"Me." Veronica chews on her lip for a moment, her eyes fixed on her plate. "I told Dr. Daphne I wish I could just start college now."

"Now?" I ask.

"Yeah." She shrugs. "I miss school, but going back to the Academy like nothing happened? It's gonna be so hard. What if everyone stares at us? Or asks questions we can't—or don't want to—answer?"

"Did Dr. Daphne have any advice?" The three of us do this every night. Talk about something good. Something bad. Something that's bothering us.

V pulls a single piece of pepperoni off her last slice and stares at it for a second. "To practice saying, 'I can't talk about that.' Or, 'I don't want to talk about that. Can we change the subject?'" With a sigh, she flops back in the chair. "I'm done. Connor can go now."

I want to give her a hug. Tell her she never has to go back to the Academy. Offer to home school her for the rest of the year. Or the rest of her *life*. But our first night out of the hospital, when Veronica asked if we could do this, she set the rules.

No judgement. No advice. And when someone says they're done, they're done.

So I just nudge the pizza box closer to her and trust that what we're building here—this new family we've made—is strong enough to weather any storm.

STANDING at the door with Connor, I wave as Leah pulls away from the curb. It took a full month for Veronica to ask if she could stay at Mitzi's for the night, and I'm both nervous and excited for my first night truly *alone* with Connor.

"She'll be fine, darlin'. She has her panic button and her self-defense teacher said she was top of her class." His fingers trace slow circles at the small of my back, but the tension in his shoulders? He doesn't like this any more than I do.

"I know." I lock the door and drape my arms around his neck. "Leah loves her new security system, by the way. Thank you for that."

Connor rests his forehead against mine, a move he uses for only the most serious of moments. "You know I wouldn't let her out of my sight unless I knew she was totally safe."

I do. But hearing him say the words? It's a balm to my soul.

"How do you *always* know just what I need?" I ask.

His deep laugh rumbles through his chest, and it's one of my favorite sounds. "Oh, I fuck up often enough. But lovin' you? It's as easy as breathin'."

Linking our fingers, I tug him down the hall to the

bedroom. *Our* bedroom. We never talked about it. Never put an "official" label on our relationship. But we both know what this is.

Forever.

"I'll understand if you want to wait." Connor shuts the bedroom door and tips his gaze to the bed. "But…"

I laugh, and so much of the worry and fear I've carried for weeks fades. "I am *not* wasting the perfect opportunity to get you naked, stud. And for once, V's music won't be so loud I can feel it through the floorboards."

He fastens his hands around my hips, walking me backward to the bed as his mouth plunders mine. I can't get his shirt off fast enough. Or mine, for that matter. But when I reach for the top button on his Wranglers, he slides his fingers into my hair and holds me still.

"I'm gonna take my time with you, darlin'. Worship you in all the ways you deserve."

"Oh, really?" I'm putty in his hands. Have been since our very first kiss. "Show me."

⸻

Six Months Later

Connor

"Last box, lil' bit. Where do you want it?"

Kneeling on the loft bed with a hammer in her hand, she casts a quick glance over at me. "That's Sasha. She belongs up here with me."

"Yes, ma'am." I pass her the box—it can't weigh more than two pounds—then drape my arm around Isabel's shoulders and lean down to whisper in her ear. "She's gonna be fine, darlin'."

"I'm not worried. Much." Her tone says otherwise, but I'd be a hypocrite to call her on it. This is a hell of a lot harder than I thought it'd be.

"Mom." V rolls her eyes, but she's clutching the stuffed whale to her chest like it's a shield. "It's only twenty minutes between here and home. Less the way Connor drives when he's...all intense and shit."

"Language!" Isabel says, then shakes her head. "Sorry. Habit."

Months ago, after one of the therapy sessions Veronica refuses to let her mother take her to, she admitted she sometimes swears so Isabel will correct her.

In some ways, she's more mature than anyone I've ever known. But in others? She's still a kid. One I'll protect any way I can.

"Done." Veronica sets the whale next to the mountain of pillows on the bed and climbs down the ladder. Handing me the level she was *certain* she wouldn't need, she offers me a sheepish grin. "Guess this thing *did* help. A little."

Isabel pulls a tissue from her pocket and swipes at her eyes. "Is there *anything* else you need? We could take you to dinner?"

"There's some welcome party in the dining hall," V says. "Besides, you'll be back here on Saturday for parents' weekend."

Parents. Plural.

My girls' voices fade into the background as I peer up at the photos hung in a perfectly straight line. Veronica and Isabel laughing at a water park when she was twelve. Her dad holding her, twin smiles on their faces. She couldn't have been more than six.

When I see the last one, I turn away, making a show of checking the new locks on the third-story window. She wouldn't let us see the photos she packed. Just said she'd picked the most important ones.

I never thought that would include a picture of the three of us. We flew out to Seattle to see my brother over spring break, and after dinner on the waterfront with Q and Graham, she'd passed Q her phone.

"Take a picture of us?" she asked. "With the Ferris wheel in the background?"

I stepped away, assuming "us" meant her and Isabel. Until she grabbed my hand.

"It's a *family* photo, Connor. You don't get to chicken out."

Our *first* family photo. It went up on the mantle the day we got home. And now it's here.

"Earth to Connor!" Veronica calls, tapping my shoulder. "Will you please tell Mom I'll be fine?"

Fuck. How can I? *I'm* not fine. If I could, I'd station two armed guards outside her door permanently. Clearing my throat, I turn away from the window. "Show me where all the panic buttons are, and we'll leave you be. As long as you promise to text your mom at least once tonight."

"Ugh. Overkill much?" Despite her protests, she goes around the room, pointing at each of the *ten* sensors I installed yesterday. When she finishes, hands on her hips, she asks, "Happy?"

"All right, baby girl. We'll go." Isabel hugs her daughter for a long moment. "I'm so proud of you, Veronica. I hope you know that."

V's eyes shine, and she nods. "I'll text you after dinner. Promise."

I'm about to take Isabel's hand when Veronica throws her arms around my waist with such force, I almost stumble back. "Love you," she whispers.

"Love you too, lil' bit." I have to force the words out over the lump in my throat. This is my kid in every way that counts, and parents' weekend can't come fast enough.

V tips her head up to look at me, and a single tear spills

onto her cheek. "I almost...until you told me everything you were going to do? The panic buttons, the window sensors, the self-defense classes...? I didn't think I could do this."

Fuck me. "You're gonna make a grown man cry. You know that?"

"Only fair." She gives me a wobbly smile before she lets go. "You've kinda nailed the whole 'overprotective dad' thing."

Pride wells in my chest, so much and so fast, it's hard to breathe until we're back at my truck, and Veronica's waving at us from her window.

"She'll be okay, won't she?" Isabel asks.

I nod, needing a moment before I try to speak. When the engine rumbles to life, I look over at the woman who changed my whole world. "I love you, darlin'. We're all gonna be just fine. There ain't nothin' this family can't do."

THANK you for reading Rogue Survivor. This is—by far—the most emotional book I have ever written. I cried for *days* while writing it. I don't know why Connor, Isabel, and Veronica affected me so much more than most, but I have a feeling they're going to stay with me for a very long time.

I hope you'll consider leaving a review wherever you purchased this book. Reviews—even short ones—are so important to your favorite authors. You don't have to write much. A single sentence or two about how the book made you feel is plenty! If you can leave a brief review, I'd appreciate it so very much.

The next book in the Gone Rogue series is available for pre-order now! Rogue Defender features washed-up, has-been, recovering alcoholic, former-CIA agent Leo Basher. (If you read Call Sign: Redemption, you might remember him.)

Leo's been drifting. Unsure what to do with the rest of his

life now that he's being forced out of the CIA. Until he meets a mysterious, woman on the run. She has information that could prevent her country—Panama—from descending into war. If she lives long enough to deliver it.

Can a man ravaged by time, torture, and his own demons find the strength to protect this brave woman from an entire army?

Find out in Rogue Defender!

As always, you can find out the latest information about all of my books and upcoming plans through my newsletter or my Unstoppable Forces reader group on Facebook!

ACKNOWLEDGMENTS

This book was hard for me. Very hard. Harder than any other book I've written.

I'm not sure why.

I spent weeks trying to convince Connor and Isabel to talk to me. I agonized over the stuff Veronica shared with me.

And I whined to everyone who would listen. Lauren, Sam, Jayne, and Jill...I couldn't have done this without you.

ABOUT THE AUTHOR

Patricia D. Eddy writes romance for the beautifully broken. Fueled by coffee, wine, and Doctor Who episodes on repeat, she brings damaged heroes and heroines together to find their happy ever afters in many different worlds. From military to paranormal to BDSM, her characters are unstoppable forces colliding with such heat, sparks always fly.

Patricia makes her home in Seattle with her husband and very spoiled cats, and when she's not writing, she loves working on home improvement projects, especially if they involve power tools.

Her award-winning *Away From Keyboard* series will always be her first love, because that's where she realized the characters in her head were telling their own stories—and she was just writing them down.

You can reach Patricia all over the web...
patriciadeddy.com
patricia@patriciadeddy.com

facebook.com/patriciadeddyauthor

twitter.com/patriciadeddy

instagram.com/patriciadeddy

bookbub.com/profile/patricia-d-eddy

tiktok.com/@patriciadeddyauthor

ALSO BY PATRICIA D. EDDY

Away From Keyboard

Dive into a steamy mix of geekery and military prowess with the men and women of Hidden Agenda and Second Sight.

Breaking His Code

In Her Sights

On His Six

Second Sight

By Lethal Force

Fighting For Valor

Finding Their Forevers (a holiday short story)

Call Sign: Redemption

Braving His Past

Protecting His Target

Defending His Hope

Gone Rogue (an Away From Keyboard spinoff series)

Rogue Protector

Rogue Officer

Rogue Survivor

Rogue Defender

Dark PNR

These novellas will take you into the darker side of the paranormal with vampires, witches, angels, demons, and more.

Forever Kept

Immortal Hunter

Wicked Omens

Storm of Sin

By the Fates

Check out the COMPLETE By the Fates series if you love dark and steamy tales of witches, devils, and an epic battle between good and evil.

By the Fates, Freed

Destined: A By the Fates Story

By the Fates, Fought

By the Fates, Fulfilled

In Blood

If you love hot Italian vampires and and a human who can hold her own against beings far stronger, then the In Blood series is for you.

Secrets in Blood

Revelations in Blood

Holidays and Heroes

Beauty isn't only skin deep and not all scars heal. Come swoon over sexy vets and the men and women who love them.

Mistletoe and Mochas

Love and Libations

Restrained

Do you like to be tied up? Or read about characters who do? Enjoy a fresh COMPLETE BDSM series that will leave you begging for more.

In His Silks

Christmas Silks

All Tied Up For New Year's

In His Collar